A Shadow of Light

A Shade of Vampire, Book 4

Bella Forrest

Also by Bella Forrest:

A SHADE OF VAMPIRE SERIES:

Derek & Sofia's story:

A Shade of Vampire (Book 1)
A Shade of Blood (Book 2)
A Castle of Sand (Book 3)
A Shadow of Light (Book 4)
A Blaze of Sun (Book 5)
A Gate of Night (Book 6)
A Break of Day (Book 7)

Note: Derek and Sofia's story completes in Book 7 of the series: *A Break of Day*, and the characters embark on entirely new adventures from Book 8 (*A Shade of Novak*).

Rose & Caleb's story:

A Shade of Novak (Book 8)
A Bond of Blood (Book 9)
A Spell of Time (Book 10)
A Chase of Prey (Book 11)
A Shade of Doubt (Book 12)
A Turn of Tides (Book 13)
A Dawn of Strength (Book 14)
A Fall of Secrets (Book 15)
An End of Night (Book 16)

A SHADE OF KIEV TRILOGY:

A Shade of Kiev 1
A Shade of Kiev 2
A Shade of Kiev 3

BEAUTIFUL MONSTER DUOLOGY:

Beautiful Monster 1
Beautiful Monster 2

For an updated list of Bella's books,
please visit www.bellaforrest.net

Join my VIP email list and I'll personally send you
an email reminder as soon as my next book is out!
Visit www.forrestbooks.com to sign up.

Contents

Prologue: Camilla

"I am going to kill him!"

Never had I been so frustrated than when I'd met Aiden Claremont during a month-long dig deep in the jungles of Cuba. From the first day we'd arrived, he had proven to be the most annoying, arrogant, conceited man who ever walked the planet and the fact that he was after the Red Orb—*my* artifact—was just one of the many things that made him a jackass in my book.

"How dare he?" I screamed as I threw a fist in the air.

"What's got your panties all up in a twist, Camilla?" my assistant and best friend, Amelia Hudson, asked me as she lifted her black-rimmed glasses over the bridge of her nose.

"That pompous, irritating, self-absorbed…" I searched my mind for a word bad enough to describe Aiden Claremont and, failing miserably to find one, I ended up with, "Doorknob."

"Doorknob?" Amelia chuckled. "*That's* the best you can come up with? Doorknob?" She rolled her eyes at me. "Aiden Claremont may be a lot of things, but he is too fine a man to deserve being called a doorknob." She got to her feet and walked to one end of our tent to make herself a cup of coffee. "What happened this time?"

I stomped my foot and crossed my arms over my chest, hating the idea of having to recount to my best friend the reason behind my ire.

Amelia finished making her coffee and plopped herself onto one of the bean bags we brought with us. She took a sip from her coffee and raised a brow at me. "Well?"

"I don't want to answer your question." I pouted.

"You're acting like a child, Cam. What's going on?"

"I hate him!"

"Yes. You made that perfectly clear from the very first moment you laid eyes on him, and yet he's all you seem to talk about."

"That's because if I don't vent, I might snap his neck."

"Right. Don't forget the last time you…"

"Shut up, Amelia." I glared at her, knowing full well what episode she was going to point out. It had been one of those cold nights at our camp and for some reason Aiden had decided to pay us a visit. We'd been in front of the campfire and he'd been as pleasant as a jerk like him was capable of. We'd ended up alone, with everyone else retiring to their tents to rest. He offered me his jacket when he noticed I was shivering. I declined, but he insisted. I couldn't even remember our conversation that night, but it somehow ended with him kissing me. When our lips parted, I motioned to slap him in the face, but he caught my arm, so I tried to slap him with my other hand, which he also caught. With him gripping both my hands, he once again kissed me. I resisted until I found myself giving in.

It was perhaps why I hated him so much—when I was around him, no matter how I tried, all my defenses crumbled around me. Aiden Claremont made me feel vulnerable and yet protected at the same time. I wasn't used to feeling that way. That scared me.

Amelia couldn't keep the grin off of her face. "When are you going to admit it, Camilla? You're into him."

"That is not true."

"Keep telling yourself that."

"He found the Orb. They're packing up camp as we speak."

"What?" Amelia spat her coffee out. "When? How?"

My shoulders sagged in defeat. "I don't know."

I could still remember the glint of amusement in his eyes as he'd winked and said, "Guess I won, Camilla. Don't worry... I'm sure you'll make for better competition next time."

The nerve of him.

Truth be told, I wasn't sure what was frustrating me more: the fact that he'd found the artifact first, or the fact that I would never see him again.

* * *

"What do you mean someone else found it?"

I couldn't look Mr. Banks in the eye. He was the private collector who'd recruited me to find the Red Orb. He'd been so excited about the artifact, recounting rumors about its dark, mysterious powers. Being an archaeologist with a deep love for adventure, I hadn't been able to resist the idea of an all-expenses-paid expedition that would lead me to some trinket probably worth less than what the adventure cost.

I didn't believe in magic or vampires or even superstition. I just wanted to get away from museums and laboratories into the field. This particular artifact was one I hadn't heard of, so I'd be discovering something new.

However, I was also skeptical about going on the expedition. Mr. Banks was said to be a hard man to work with. He wanted returns for his investments and was known to have a bad temper when he didn't get what he wanted.

Thus, as I sat across from him on one of the couches in the lounge area of his office, I was desperately trying to figure out how to explain that someone had got to the Orb before I did.

"There was another crew digging at the site. They were also after the Orb."

"And who, might I ask, is behind this other crew?"

His name tasted bitter in my mouth. "Aiden Claremont."

Mr. Banks' wrinkled old face contorted in surprise. "Aiden Claremont? What would a guy like him want with an artifact like that?"

I frowned, raising my eyes to meet his for the first time. "You know him?"

"Of course I know him." The man was looking at me like I'd been living under a rock all my life. "He's one of the youngest multimillionaires in the world. He owns one of the largest security conglomerates in the United States. You've never heard of him?"

I shook my head. "Hard to hear about people like that when you spend all your time inside libraries and museums."

Mr. Banks narrowed his eyes on me. "Well, we had a deal, Miss Saunders. I pay for your dig, you get me the Orb. Unless you get the Red Orb into my hands, then I'll ask you to pay me back everything I spent on your expedition."

I gripped the armrests of my seat. There was no way I could afford to part with that kind of money. "But how... Where would I get that much money?"

"Figure it out. I'll give you a month, Miss Saunders."

* * *

Mr. Banks' ultimatum was still circling my mind when I returned to the apartment I was sharing with Amelia. The moment I arrived, she threw a pillow at me.

"You'll never guess who just called," she said.

"Not in the mood for guessing games." I went straight for the refrigerator to get the pink lemonade I'd made earlier that day. "I have a headache."

"What happened?"

"I don't want to talk about it."

"All right. Well, you'll be happy to find out that the love of your life, Aiden Claremont, just called. He's hoping to meet you for dinner tonight."

I choked on the lemonade—something Amelia found hilarious, especially after she had taken a quick shot of the scene with her Polaroid camera. "I knew your reaction to the news would be precious."

"Why would he want to meet for dinner?" I asked, feeling my cheeks grow red at the prospect of seeing him again. I inwardly slapped myself for acting like a foolish teenager.

"How am I supposed to know?" Amelia shrugged. "Oh, my gosh, Cam. Are you blushing?"

"I'm not!" But I was.

* * *

I checked my appearance in the living room's full-length mirror for about the hundredth time. I didn't understand why I cared what he thought about me. I reminded myself that I hated him, that he was an arrogant, pompous and conceited "doorknob," but I was fooling myself and I knew it. Aiden Claremont was every bit my match.

Plus he has the Red Orb. Of course I find him attractive, I told myself as I smoothed my palms over my waist. I wasn't exactly the kind of girl one would find in magazines, with the tall, skinny figure. I had more of an athletic build—mostly because of the kind of work I did. Still, I knew I was beautiful. As I stared at myself in the mirror, taking in what others often called my assets, a familiar sickening sensation came over me.

For all the glory it got from the world, beauty was a commodity that I'd had to pay dearly for. Long-buried memories of my past began to haunt me and I had to hold on to a nearby chair for support.

"Wow, Cam." Amelia stepped out of her bedroom. "Are you all right? Nervous about your date?"

"It's not a date."

"Uh-huh. You'll be making a bunch of little Aidens and Camillas in no time."

The idea revolted me. "No. Never. Mark my words, Amelia. I will never have children—his or anyone else's."

* * *

I never forgot the way Aiden looked that night in that crisp white shirt, those straight-cut jeans, those shiny black shoes. That smile, that look in his eyes when he first laid eyes on me—like I was the most beautiful woman in the room.

"Hello, gorgeous," he greeted me with a wide smile.

I frowned at him, desperately trying to keep my walls up, afraid of what would happen once they crumbled—inevitable considering how charming he was being. "Could we just get to business, Claremont? Why did you ask to meet with me?"

"Get to business, Camilla? Is that why you put on mascara to emphasize those lovely long lashes of yours? Is that why you're all dolled up and looking incredible tonight?" He narrowed his eyes at me. "You dressed up just so we could discuss business?"

"The way I look and the way I dress should be of no concern to you, Claremont." I shifted on my seat, hoping that my voice wouldn't break. "I want the Red Orb. What do I have to do to get it?"

That infuriating smirk of his formed on his lips. "I don't know. What are you willing to do to get it?"

I was half-expecting his ego to make his head explode. Annoyed, I heaved a sigh and stood up. "This is such a waste of time."

"No, wait." He laid a hand on my shoulder. "I'm sorry. Let's try that again."

I looked into his eyes, seeing his sincerity. "Try *what* again?"

"Try to have a civilized conversation, Cam. I promise to be less of a jerk." He raised one hand in the air to make his pledge official. "Hear me out."

I kept my eyes on him as I slowly sat back on my chair. "Don't give me any more of your crap, Claremont," I warned.

"No more of that." He sat back down and cleared his throat.

He asked if we should order first and I nodded. We made our orders—an awkward ordeal—before I once again eyed him for some sort of explanation for our meeting.

He took a deep breath after the waiter left. "So you want the Red Orb?"

"I told you that."

"I'll give it to you."

My brow quirked up. "Just like that?"

He slowly nodded. "Yeah. Just like that."

"That doesn't make sense. You've been driving me crazy over the past few weeks trying to get a hold of that artifact. Now you're just going to give it to me?"

"Well, first of all, you have to admit that the competition made the dig a whole lot more fun. Messing with you was the most fun I had during that whole expedition. Your reaction gave me far more satisfaction than actually getting the Orb," he admitted with an chuckle.

"I'm glad you were entertained." I feigned annoyance, even though a smile was threatening to form on my lips as memories of all the bickering and banter I'd had with him came to mind.

"Look." He tilted his head to the side. "I'm a guy who knows what he wants. I traveled to Cuba wanting the Orb and I got it, but I realized that there's something I want more than the Orb."

I was afraid to ask, but the words came out of my mouth before I could hold them back. "And what's that?"

"You, Camilla."

* * *

That was the first date among many that followed after we got back to the States. I fell in love with Aiden Claremont, so when he proposed to me after several weeks of dating, I couldn't say no.

Truth be told, I was terrified. Throughout the time we were dating, we were never intimate. I told him that I wanted to wait until marriage and he respected that. The fact that he respected my choice to wait made me admire him even more, but it also made me dread the night I had to be intimate with him.

On the night of our honeymoon, I wanted desperately to please him, to be the blushing bride eager to share a bed with her doting husband, but no matter how I tried to take pleasure in his touch, I couldn't. I pretended on his behalf, but the moment he fell asleep, cradling me in his arms, I burst into tears.

I was far too damaged by my past to ever enjoy such pleasures.

Of course, Aiden was no fool. He knew something was wrong. He noticed times when I would shut down whenever he tried to make love to me, but I always avoided answering his questions about it. My past was my own nightmare to live with. He didn't need to share the burden.

The first few months of our marriage were the best months of my life. Aiden was everything I could ask for in a man. He was loving and affectionate. He made me want to be the best I could be for him. I was satisfied, but I knew that he wasn't, or at least he wouldn't be for long.

Whenever he brought up the topic of children, I skirted around it. I didn't want him to know that I never wanted to have children. I kept taking birth control pills without his knowledge;

thus, it came as a complete surprise to me when, several months after our honeymoon, I became pregnant. I kicked myself for allowing Aiden to come with me to the checkup. If he hadn't been there—if I hadn't seen the delight in his eyes when he found out, if I hadn't seen for myself how much joy I would bring him by carrying the child—I would've immediately had an abortion. Sofia never would've been born.

The day our daughter was born, I knew from the way Aiden stared at her that I had just lost him. I no longer held all of his heart. A great big chunk of it had just been taken from me by Sofia.

* * *

Sofia grew lovelier each year. She was precious to me, because she was precious to him. Still, I was terrified. Though Aiden remained a wonderful husband to me, and though he still looked at me the same way he'd looked at me on our first date, I didn't want him to love Sofia more than he loved me.

I was afraid of being abandoned. Every father-daughter outing they went on brought me into despair Aiden could never understand. Never did I feel more weak than when Aiden spent time alone with Sofia, time I was convinced should've been mine. I would've preferred to keep Sofia to myself than to have her be with her father. Aiden mistook this as me being selfish with Sofia and often teased me about it, but in reality, it was me being selfish with him.

I was getting obsessed with the man I loved and, through the years, I began to notice little things about him that convinced me that he would eventually leave me. Sofia, after all, was the only girl he needed in his life. She had taken my place.

I began to notice Aiden's hushed conversations over the phone, prolonged out-of-town trips and extra hours at work. These things were normal for him, considering the demands of his work, but as time wore on, I was convinced that he was having an affair. I tried to convince myself that I was just being paranoid, but I couldn't help myself. One night, when nine-year-old Sofia was already tucked in bed, I eavesdropped on a conversation Aiden was having over the phone.

He spoke in hushed tones. "The Maslen vampires are gaining power. We can't have that." A slew of curses escaped his lips. "Damn it. Track him down. Borys Maslen was last seen in Egypt. Find him and destroy him."

The first thought that came to mind was: *Aiden has gone mad. How could anybody in their right mind believe in vampires?* But I knew Aiden. He was perhaps the most intelligent and rational man I'd ever had the pleasure of meeting. When it came to his work, he wasn't one to believe in any nonsense.

I tried to excuse what I had heard by rationalizing that perhaps Aiden was just talking in some sort of corporate code. Perhaps "vampires" was just code for their competition.

I didn't know how it happened, but it became an obsession. Much as I hated it, I began to eavesdrop on Aiden's conversations about vampires and Egypt and the Maslens. At some point, I couldn't take it anymore. I began doing research. I contacted old friends of mine from libraries and told them that I was interested in anything they knew about vampires. I gave them some excuse about wanting to write a novel.

The newfound interest wasn't something I couldn't keep from

my husband, so when he confronted me about it, I had a ready answer. "I think they exist. Don't you?"

I was waiting for him to lie, to laugh me off and tell me that I was being crazy, but no, he lifted one of the books I was reading and began thumbing through its pages. "Of course they exist."

I narrowed my eyes at him. "You... Aiden Claremont... actually believe in vampires?"

He shrugged one shoulder as he placed the book he was thumbing through back on my work desk. "After a decade of marriage, my lovely Camilla, there are still a lot of things about me you don't know."

"Tell me then."

"I don't know if I should, Cam. Why are you so interested in them all of a sudden?"

"How can I not be interested?" I shrugged. "They're fascinating, and now you tell me that you actually believe in them. Can you blame me for being intrigued?"

I was expecting a quip about how he loved my adventurous side. Instead he just shook his head. "There's nothing fascinating about vampires, Cam. They are the most vile creatures to ever walk the planet. Powerful, but evil beyond measure... Stay away from them."

His admonition only served to make me more curious. I began quizzing Aiden about what he knew about vampires and why on earth he knew so much about them. He willingly told me what he knew, but always kept silent about how he'd found out. I hated that he was keeping things from me. It made me feel betrayed that my husband had this mysterious connection with vampires that he had never told me about, but I didn't voice it.

At some point, he got irritated about all the questions about vampires. He especially hated it when I mentioned them when Sofia was around.

"Cam, I'm warning you. I don't ever want Sofia to be exposed to these monsters. I don't even want her to know about them. If I could, I'd remove everything in this world that points to the existence of these creatures. I would do everything possible to keep our daughter away from them."

I barely even understood what he was saying at that time. I couldn't understand his hatred toward vampires or why he was so adamant about keeping his family away from those creatures. Whenever I thought of vampires, all I could think of was the power that came with them. I wanted that power.

I began asking Aiden about how to find vampires, how to track them down. During times when he obviously did not want to talk about vampires, I would turn on my charm and usually after a tumble in bed, he would oblige me and answer my questions.

I might not have realized it at first, but I saw the vampires as my escape from the hopelessness brought about by my own daughter's birth. I was tired of feeling so powerless against all the despair and all the fears, and the fascination I felt for those dark creatures began to consume me.

When I felt ready to hunt for a vampire, I asked Aiden if I could start working as an archaeologist once again. Of course, he didn't deny this request. He even encouraged it.

"I was wondering when you would once again give in to that adventurous streak I know you have," he said as he kissed me on the forehead. "Maybe you'll think less about vampires and more about archaeology." He seemed so pleased as he held me in his arms and kissed me.

I realized then that my love for him was the reason I was so weak.

Two weeks after that, I was off to my first adventure in years. My destination, of course, was Egypt.

* * *

I was determined not to leave Egypt until I found out whether Borys Maslen was what I suspected—a vampire. It took a couple of weeks of digging and prodding, following the tips and tricks I'd learned to track down vampires, before the man I was looking for came to me.

It was the middle of the night and I had just crawled into my bed when a hand clamped over my mouth and the weight of a man fell atop me. At first, I thought I was about to be assaulted, but when fangs flashed, my emotions shifted from terror to fascination.

"I know you've been looking for me, woman," he hissed into my ear. "Why is that? Choose your answer well, for it may be your last. And don't you dare scream, or your death will be a slow one."

He took his hand away from my mouth. I looked right into his face, unflinching. "I want to become a vampire."

At that, he scoffed. "You? A vampire?"

"Yes."

"Why on earth would I give you that honor?"

"I'll give you anything, do anything…"

His face broke into a manic smile, his dark eyes glimmering against the lamp's dim light. "Anything? Prove your loyalty to me by giving me the person most precious to you."

"If I do, what are you going to do to them?"

"Whatever I please."

The most precious person in my life was and would always be Aiden. For a moment, I considered giving him to this stranger, this *vampire*, but I couldn't. My love for him overpowered my desire to become like the powerful creature that had found me that night. However, there was one person precious in my life whom I could offer to him. "I have a daughter. She's nine years old. I'm willing to offer her up to you to prove my loyalty."

The recollection of the delighted smile on his face would still send chills up my spine many years later.

"Perfect," he said, before biting into my neck, injecting the serum that would forever destroy Camilla Claremont and bring Ingrid Maslen into being.

* * *

I tried to convince myself that I never felt regret after that night. As Ingrid Maslen, I was immortal, I was powerful and I had a family of vampires who would never leave me. I would never again be abandoned.

I did a good job pretending that I was all right, but many years later, I realized that I wasn't.

I was in inner turmoil as my daughter hissed at Borys, "I'm *not* your betrothed." She spoke the words as if it was the most sickening notion she'd ever contemplated.

That was my cue. I braced myself to face Sofia for the first time since I had offered her up as prey for a vampire to feast on. "Actually, Sofia," I spoke up as I stepped out of the curtains and took my place beside Borys' throne, "you really are his betrothed."

No words could explain the way I felt upon seeing the shock and grief on her face when she laid eyes on me. I wanted to wipe her tears away. I wanted to pull her into my arms and embrace her.

Seeing what a beauty my daughter had become—lovelier than I ever was at eighteen years old—it hit me full force what I had given up when I became Ingrid Maslen.

I'd given my daughter up. I'd given my husband up. I'd given my entire life up.

"She looks so happy to see you, Ingrid." Borys tilted his head to the side, a manic smile on his face.

Sofia's eyes were fixed on me. She couldn't have possibly known the effect it had on me when she uttered, "Mom?"

I hated that I felt affection toward Sofia, but it was the truth nonetheless: I detested the idea of him touching my daughter. The thought made me sick to my stomach. I knew the things he would put her through. I'd seen him do it to countless young women, and I didn't want that for her, but I belonged to Borys and I knew it. Thus Sofia belonged to him too.

Not knowing how to handle my feelings, I did the only thing I could: I inched closer to the dark side.

Thus, I was able to smile at her—indifferent to her plight—and tell her, "Yes, Sofia. It's me. Your mother. I betrothed you to Borys a long time ago. You are rightfully his."

* * *

I stood by Sofia's bed as the blood trickled down her milky white thighs. Her legs were quivering from the pain. She was obviously trying to fight back the tears. She gave me a quick look—accusing, hurt and full of contempt. I couldn't blame her. I would've hated myself too had I been in her place.

I stood by and watched her scream as Borys kissed her at the same time he sank his claws into her thighs, drawing blood. I did nothing. As I watched him do as he pleased with her, all I could think about was what she had just revealed to us—that she was already married to Derek Novak.

A part of me still hoped that I would see her in a white gown walking down the aisle to her groom. *I missed it. I missed my own daughter's wedding.*

When Borys threatened to kill Derek so that he could take his rightful place as Sofia's husband, I was overwhelmed with relief. *I can still be there at her wedding.*

My stomach clenched at my own sick thinking, but before guilt could creep in, Borys pushed Sofia to the ground and looked my way to instruct me to heal my daughter. I was transfixed by the sight of Sofia whimpering on the ground. I had no idea what to do. I wanted to ease her pain. Yet another part of me just wanted to get as far away from her as possible.

I ordered two guards to help me take her to her bedroom.

"Be gentle with her," I snapped at them. "She is, after all, to become your queen."

They gave me strange glances, but I ignored them and walked ahead to the bedroom.

Later, I had vampire blood brought to her in order for the wounds on her legs to heal.

"You've drunk vampire blood before," I told her, noticing drinking blood didn't seem to faze her at all.

She just glared at me. That was when I realized that she wasn't like me at all. I'd thought that she was weak—and from her appearance alone, it seemed that way—but underneath her shaking exterior, I could only sense one thing from Sofia: power.

Intimidated, I tried to break her down the next time I encountered her. Borys sent me to bring her to his chambers. I wondered if he was being cruel or if he was testing my loyalty. I found the idea ridiculous. Hadn't I already proven how loyal I was to him?

In Sofia's bedroom, I found her speaking to her best friend, Ben—Amelia's son. I found myself missing my best friend, who'd been there for me during some of the toughest days of my life while I'd still been Camilla Claremont. I hated looking at Ben because of how much he reminded me of Amelia.

"I want time alone with my daughter," I told the guards. "Have the young man brought to the little blonde vampire from The Shade. She's been harping on about him since she got here."

The atmosphere tensed as I watched the look of horror on Sofia's face. For some reason, I found delight in evoking terror in her.

"No..." Sofia begged. "Please... no... Not her... Not Claudia... Mother, please."

Mother. The word was like a splash of cold water—a final plea for me to show the affection my daughter was clearly starving for. I raised a hand toward the guards, who were already approaching to take Ben. "Wait. What did you just call me?"

"Mother..." Sofia's lips trembled as she spoke. She grabbed Ben's hand, seeming to both give and draw strength from him. "Isn't that what you are? My mother?"

"Yes. That's right, Sofia." I smiled. "I'm your mother." The powerful Ingrid would always win over weak and pathetic Camilla. "That means you do what I say, right?"

She nodded. "Of course."

"So you're not going to cause any trouble tomorrow?"

"Tomorrow?" Her grip on Ben's hand tightened.

"Yes. Tomorrow. You're to be wed to Borys tomorrow."

"Why? Why would you do this? Why would you force your own daughter to marry that brute?"

I began brushing strands of her hair away from her face. "You just don't know him, Sofia. Borys deserves the best and you, Sofia, are the best. Why wouldn't you be? You're my blood, my beautiful, perfect little girl. You belong to Borys." I straightened to my full height. "I've changed my mind," I announced. "Leave the boy here. The Shade's little blonde vampire can have him after the wedding. Right now, Borys is requesting the presence of his blooming bride. Have my daughter brought to his chambers."

I watched as the guards dragged my daughter away to whatever fate Borys had for her. I watched wondering why I was so threatened by her. I watched hoping that she would break down, because the strength of her spirit only highlighted the weakness of mine.

* * *

One would have to be blind not to see how much Sofia loved the legendary Derek Novak, rumored to be the most powerful vampire alive, king of The Shade, the largest and most influential vampire coven in existence. The look on his face upon seeing her made it quite evident that he felt the same way.

Their reunion would haunt me my whole life. The way they

whispered comfort into each other's ears and caressed one another would forever be etched into my mind.

I had hoped that I would experience the same thing upon seeing Aiden, but when the hunters attacked and our eyes met for the first time in almost a decade, all I could see was pure and utter hatred.

I still loved Aiden Claremont, but he no longer felt the same way about me. I couldn't blame him, but I hated that he still looked at Sofia as if he worshiped the ground she walked on.

Whatever love I felt for my daughter faded away when Aiden chose to ride in her helicopter instead of mine. The hunters wanted me dead, but Aiden stopped them. I thought it was because he still cared, but he gave me one glare and coldly said, "I want her dead too, but my daughter isn't about to lose a mother. Not tonight."

Everything had to be about her.

Sofia had ruined my life. Not only that, but the world of all these powerful men seemed to revolve around her—Aiden, Derek, even Borys. I was jealous of her.

Sofia was beautiful inside and out. She had a good heart and an inexplicable strength of spirit. She was powerful and vied for as the immune—a human who could never be turned into a vampire. She was loved.

Sofia was everything that I was not. Whenever I laid eyes on her after that fateful night when The Oasis was destroyed and we were all taken to enemy territory—to the hunters' headquarters— three words went through my mind.

I hate you.

Chapter 1: Derek

Blindfolded, I was enveloped by pitch blackness. Tucked between two hunters in the back seat of a black SUV, my wrists tied together in front of me, I found the ride bumpy and uncomfortable.

As we'd left the hunters' headquarters, I couldn't help but smirk when the hunters bound my wrists together.

Do they really think I can't just snap off whatever they bind me with?

Still, not wanting to give them any reason to harm me, I'd let them have their way. I couldn't afford to cross the hunters—not while I was in their territory, not when I was at their mercy.

The ride was excruciatingly long, and now that we were outside headquarters, I was gearing myself up for a fight. I was fully expecting them to try to kill me. It didn't take a genius to realize that every single one of the four hunters escorting me out of hawk territory hated me.

I wasn't surprised. I knew that they resented Aiden for not ending my life just because his daughter was in love with me. I also knew that Aiden letting me go was too good to be true. He was the head hunter—with a deep-seated hatred for vampires.

They're either going to kill me or they're going to follow me to The Shade. The Shade was the island I had given my life to protect. If the hunters ever found the island, it would be the end of arguably the most powerful vampire coven in the world—the Novak coven, *my* coven. I couldn't have that. However, I found it impossible to come up with a plan—not when I couldn't get my mind off of Sofia.

I had already convinced myself that it was the right thing to do to leave Sofia behind. She was safe with her father, safer than she would be with me. I swallowed hard, once again keenly aware of my hunger for her, the taste of her blood still lingering in my mouth.

Sofia—my fiancée, the only woman I had ever loved—was the immune. *How is it possible that she cannot turn into a vampire? How could she be immune to this wretched curse?*

Flashbacks of the night she had told me of her past haunted me. I hated Borys. I hated her mother for allowing everything to happen. I wondered what it all meant—her being the immune.

I grimaced. *It means that she can never be immortal like I am. It means that despite all my proclamations that I would someday marry her, she was right all along. We can never really be together.*

I shoved thoughts of her away. If I was going to survive that night, I needed to think about how to get the hunters off my back and get to The Shade without being followed.

There wasn't much time for me to think.

"We're here, your highness," the hunter on my right side drawled.

The sound of doors opening was followed by hands dragging me out of the car. My feet had just hit what felt like gravel when one of the hunters whispered, "I say we kill him."

The statement was followed by a punch in the gut and a wooden stake through my left arm.

I steeled myself against the throbbing pain, snapped the rope they used to bind my wrists together and pulled my blindfold off before glaring at my captors.

"You really shouldn't have done that."

Shock dawned on their faces. Their reactions made it clear that it wasn't normal for vampires to be able to get out of those ropes. Some sort of spell had most likely been placed on those ropes by the hunters' witches.

Recovering from their shock, all four reached for their weapons as I pulled out the wooden stake from my arm. The quickest among the four already had his UV-ray gun out. His swiftness was his death, because I threw the wooden stake, the weapon digging through his skull.

Sofia's blood coursed through me, and its amazing powers lit me up. Flashes of her green eyes, her auburn hair, her inviting smile filled my mind and her influence on me took over. I used my agility to get behind one of the hunters to take hold of his head, threatening to snap his neck. The stab wound on my arm had already healed.

"There doesn't have to be any more bloodshed." I eyed the other two men. They were exchanging glances.

"I don't mind dying." The hunter in my arms spoke up. "End him. End Derek Novak. What could Aiden do to punish you? He probably secretly hoped that we'd do it."

I raised a brow, taken aback. *So Aiden didn't order my execution.* "He may not mind dying, but I really mind having to kill all three of you."

One of the hunters—a man with a bald head and tattoos running down his neck and arms—glared at me. "No vampire has ever been able to break those ropes before."

"I'm stronger than most vampires." Cora had made sure of that. After I'd established The Shade, she'd put me into a four-hundred-year slumber and, to ensure that I'd be able to fulfill the prophecy spoken about me, she'd added a spell that would make me stronger and stronger as I slumbered.

"What do you propose we do?" the tattooed hunter asked.

"What do you mean what do we do?" my hostage admonished. "You kill him!"

The other two ignored him. They kept their eyes on me, waiting for a response.

I took a quick look at our surroundings. We were in some sort of woods. "Toss me the keys to the SUV. I want your wallets too. Where's the highway?"

The tattooed hunter tossed the keys to me and pointed toward the direction of the highway. Within minutes, I was driving in the hunters' black SUV, with the hunters' wallets in the passenger seat beside me. I had no idea where I was or where I was going, but I still had a tank full of gas and a long road ahead of me.

I couldn't help but recall the last time I'd driven a car—a red convertible. Sofia had been in the passenger's seat, screaming, certain that I was about to drive her to her death. She'd declared that day my birthday, refusing to accept the idea that I no longer needed to celebrate the day I was born.

The reality of what I had just done sank into me. I'd left Sofia. I hadn't even said goodbye. I'd left in the middle of the night, taking in the peaceful sight of her asleep for as long as I could, before the hunters had taken me away.

I began to feel it immediately, the familiar forces of the darkness beginning to break down my defenses.

Sofia was my light and I was driving away from her—far away.

I gripped the steering wheel. *I can't let the darkness take over. Not again. I must find a way to survive apart from Sofia.* I kept her in my mind, recalling every precious memory I had of her. *If I lose sight of her, it will be the end of us all.*

Chapter 2: Sofia

"Sofia, he's busy! You can't just barge into his office without being called for." Zinnia Wolfe folded her arms.

But I couldn't care less. "Watch me. I'm his daughter and I deserve an explanation."

I barged inside what I knew was off limits for guests like me, knowing that of all the places in the giant estate known as Hawk Headquarters, I was most likely to find my father there.

"You can't go in there!" Zinnia ran after me.

I halted only when I was already inside the control center. It was the first time I had ever entered this part of the headquarters. I was shocked by what I saw. Almost like a newsroom, the control center was decked with advanced technology, with dozens upon dozens of hunters milling around the room, keeping track on what seemed like a network of at least a hundred computers tracking heaven knew what.

"Too late," I told Zinnia, who was catching her breath beside me. My father was pointing at a giant flatscreen monitor. He looked upset about something.

"Vampires are easier to get a hold of than you," Zinnia hissed. She tried to grab my arm, but I was already on the move toward my father.

The moment Aiden realized that I was storming toward him, I could no longer keep my temper in check. "Where is he? What have you done to him?" I yelled.

"Sorry... I couldn't stop her," Zinnia apologized. Aiden had assigned her to keep an eye on me from the moment I arrived with Derek at the headquarters.

Aiden looked around the control room before slightly bowing his head and glaring at me. "Sofia, don't make a scene. We can talk about this elsewhere."

"I don't care where we talk or who hears us. I want to know where Derek is!"

"I don't know where. He left of his own free will, Sofia."

"You liar." I shook my head furiously. "Derek would never leave me. Not unless you did something to make him leave. He would never!"

I was trembling. Nothing my father could tell me would convince me that Derek would leave me here. Yet deep inside, I was afraid that it was true. *He's forever immortal and I am mortal. Perhaps he thought that it was better for us to be apart.* I shook the thought away. *No. Derek wouldn't do that to me. He wouldn't abandon me.*

My father took a deep breath. "Come with me. Let's go to my office."

As we both followed Aiden, Zinnia threw curious glances my way.

"What?" I asked her, unable to reel in the foul mood I was in. I couldn't help it. I was panicking inside.

"I just…" She shook her head. "Never mind."

"Just spit it out, Zinnia."

She hesitated, but said, "What's so special about you? They're all enamored by you. Derek, Ben, Borys, Lucas…"

I met her gaze and smiled bitterly. "I haven't got a clue."

That was a lie. I knew why they wanted me. Borys wanted me because he was a sick bastard who thought that he owned me and was fascinated by my immunity to the vampire's curse. Lucas had wanted me because he'd found me and brought me to The Shade. He'd also had a taste of my blood and up to his very last breath he'd craved me. Ben had wanted me because he was my best friend, and there was a time when I'd thought I'd wanted him too, but we just weren't meant to be together. I loved him though, and his death still weighed heavily on my heart.

Derek, on the other hand… he wanted me because I was in love with him and he felt the same way.

Yes, I know why they want me, but it doesn't mean I'm special. I'm just who I am and who I am is somehow entangled in all this mess.

We finally reached Aiden's office, where he motioned for me to take a seat and for Zinnia to close the door behind her.

I chose to stand as Aiden sat on the leather recliner behind the large glass desk which served as the centerpiece of the spacious office.

"You're really not going to sit down?"

I shook my head, crossing my arms over my chest.

"You remind me so much of your mother sometimes." He said it with such brokenness, I was taken aback, and I couldn't help but soften a little at the sight of his pain. Any mention of my mother was painful. I knew Ingrid was somewhere inside the headquarters—a captive of the hunters. Just thinking of her made me ache. I wasn't even sure if Aiden's claim that I reminded him of her was a good thing or not.

"You really did love her, didn't you?" It was the first time I could remember ever sharing such a personal moment with him.

Aiden smiled bitterly. He pulled a cigar from a desk drawer and lit it up before eyeing me. "So why exactly are you throwing such a fit, my lovely daughter?"

My anger rose. "Where is Derek?" I demanded.

"He's probably on his way back to his kingdom by now."

"He wouldn't leave without me."

Aiden sat straight on his seat, shoulders squared. "He told me that if he stayed here, he wouldn't be able to keep himself from drinking you dry."

My gut clenched. *How could he possibly know that Derek already drank my blood? Could Derek really have told him that?*

"I know I haven't been much of a father to you, Sofia, but why would you ever willingly feed a vampire your own blood?"

Zinnia looked at me like I was insane. "You've been feeding him your blood? What is wrong with you?"

Aiden glared at her. "Stay out of this, Zinnia."

I hated that he was acting like some sort of authority figure in my life. He didn't have that right—not after abandoning me for years, leaving me in the care of the Hudsons and barely acknowledging my existence until a few weeks ago.

"Don't." I shook my head. "Don't start acting like a father now, Aiden. I don't need to explain myself to you."

"Yes, Sofia. You do. Derek Novak is one of the most powerful vampires alive and he is craving your blood. How is this not a reason to be concerned?"

"You don't understand. We are strongest together and we are weakest apart. That may not make sense to you, but you have to realize that a life without him… for me, that's no life at all!"

I should've known that an emotional plea would just sound weak to the rational and calculating mind of Aiden Claremont. Both he and Zinnia stared at me as if I had somehow been brainwashed.

"Do you love Derek Novak?" Aiden asked after a long and awkward pause.

"Yes!" I exclaimed. "I love him. I love Derek."

"And how exactly will this work, Sofia? He's immortal. What do you intend to do? Turn into a vampire so you can be with him for all eternity? So you can be a killer like him? Do you even have any idea how many people have died in his hands?"

He was preying on my own deepest fears about my relationship with Derek. As if Derek's immortality wasn't already haunting me, my father had to rub it in my face.

"You deserve so much better than Derek Novak, Sofia."

I smiled bitterly as I shook my head. "You have no idea who Derek is, and trust me when I say this, Father… even if I wanted to, I could never become a vampire. Are you happy now?"

He narrowed his eyes. "What exactly are you saying, Sofia?"

My jaw tightened as I glared at my father. "It doesn't matter.

What matters right now is this: I am going to find out what happened to Derek, and if I find out that you were behind it, I will never forgive you."

Aiden's smirk as he shook his head and took a puff of his cigar sent chills down my spine. "No, Sofia. You aren't going anywhere near Derek. Not again. In fact, you're not going to leave this place. You will train as a hunter and learn to defend yourself against these vampires. I will keep you here until your deluded love for him is weaned out of your system."

Despite my shock, I managed to take a few steps closer. "You can't keep me prisoner here."

At that, my father scoffed. "Oh, yes, I can, darling. Yes, I can."

Chapter 3: Derek

When I reached Natalie Borgia's log cabin in the country, for the first time since I'd left the hunters' headquarters, I actually felt secure.

Natalie was an old friend of mine. She was also one of the few rogue vampires who had full access to all of the vampire covens. She was the ultimate diplomat, the main communication line between all vampire covens. She was invaluable to our kind.

I walked along the stone path that led to the log cabin and knocked on the door. When Natalie opened it, a smile spread across her face as she handed me a glass of blood.

"I'm sure you're famished." The Italian girl always had a way of making me feel taken care of.

I took the glass and drank its contents in one go. I hadn't had a drop of blood in my system since I'd left hunter territory. I hadn't been able to bear the thought of killing the humans I had come across during my journey to Natalie's safe house. I was indeed famished.

Natalie welcomed me into the cabin and asked me to make myself comfortable as she poured another glass of blood for me. As I waited for her, I recalled the first time I'd got in touch with her a couple of days back.

"Derek? What is going on? Where are you? Do you have any idea how many people are looking for you right now?"

Gripping the disposable cell phone, I'd never thought I could be as elated to hear Natalie Borgia's voice as I was at that moment. "I need you to help me get back to The Shade without the hunters following me. I've been trying to get them off my back for the past two days. It's been hell."

"Two days? Where are you? How are you keeping out of the sunlight?"

Hidden in some sleazy motel in the middle of who knew where, I was in no mood to answer her questions. "Natalie, I appreciate your concern, but right now, could you be less of a friend and more of a diplomat?"

Truth be told, I couldn't wrap my mind around how I had survived the past two days. At The Shade, both Sofia and my sister Vivienne—before she'd passed away at the hands of the hunters—had tried their best to keep me up to date with the technologies and norms of the twenty-first century. Still, living them out firsthand was a shock. The world was far different from four hundred years ago.

"Okay," Natalie said, her voice lower. "What do you want me to do?"

"The hunters know where I am at all times. I can't get them off my back no matter how hard I try."

"They probably have a tracker on you. Do you have anything on you that came from the hunters' headquarters?"

"I have credit cards, wallets, drivers' licenses, an SUV..."

I could practically see Natalie roll her eyes. "Get rid of all of those. You don't know which is being tracked, so you might as well just get rid of everything. I'm going to give you an address. That's my safe house. Don't bring anything that the hunters have been in contact with. Did you get all of that?"

I nodded before remembering that she couldn't actually see me. "Yes. Thank you."

"Get here safe, Derek. I'm worried about you."

"I will. Thanks." I heaved a deep sigh before looking at the SUV. I said goodbye to it, inwardly groaning at all the running I was about to do.

Natalie plopped on the empty space on the couch beside me as she handed me another glass of blood. "I'm glad you made it. You sure the hunters aren't still on your back?"

"I lost them a day ago. Had to take several detours though."

"What's going on, Derek? Where were you? The people at The Shade have been going mad since they heard news of the fall of The Oasis. Rumors are that you're siding with the hunters."

I almost choked on my drink. "Siding with the hunters? Did you not hear me when I said that they've been hunting me for days?"

"Well, the rumor is that they caught you and that you, Ingrid, Claudia and Sofia were taken to hunter territory. We all thought you were a goner, and yet here you are. How could you have escaped the hunters? Hunter territory is to vampires as The Shade is to humans. Once you get in, you can't get out."

I didn't like where the conversation was going. I finished the drink and laid the glass on the coffee table. "I can't believe that anyone would think that I would work with the hunters."

"Well, you were once one of the most feared hunters alive. You have to admit that coming out of hunter territory unscathed is suspicious."

"Natalie, you believe me when I say that the only reason they kept me alive was because of Sofia, right?"

"I'm a rogue, Derek. What does it matter what I believe? My job is to remain a diplomat and bring messages between covens. Since when does my opinion count?"

"It counts to me."

"Of course I believe you, but come on… It's not like the other covens will buy that story. For crying out loud, Derek, do you really expect them to believe that you walked out of hunter territory thanks to true love?"

"I expect them to believe that there is an exception to every rule. You said it yourself, Natalie… Hunter territory is to vampires as The Shade is to humans. Sofia and Ben were the exceptions. They got out of The Shade, did they not? Isn't it high time that a vampire got out of hunter territory unscathed?"

"Sure." Natalie shrugged. "I know you well enough to buy that, but just to play devil's advocate here, you are in love with Sofia Claremont, who is the daughter of the notorious Ingrid Maslen. Not only that, she's also the daughter of Aiden Claremont, or as we know him in our world, the infamous hunter, Reuben."

"What are you trying to tell me, Natalie?" I asked, growing weary of the conversation.

"Gregor and Borys are alive and no one knows where they are. Other covens are beginning to suspect the Novaks' loyalties. You appeared at The Oasis on the exact same day the hunters attacked. Some don't think that's a coincidence."

"What do you expect me to do about that?" I could practically feel the darkness coming and all I could think about was how much I wanted to hold Sofia in my arms. Just the thought of her made my heart pound, made me crave her blood. It was this blood thirst that reminded me why it had been necessary for me to leave her.

Natalie must've sensed my tension, because uncharacteristically of her, she brushed a hand over my shoulder. "All I'm saying, Novak, is that The Shade won't be safe for long. I think you should expect that the coven leaders will eventually attack the island."

I could only scoff. "Tell me something I don't know."

At that moment, I could almost envision the future and all the bloodshed ahead. I wanted to laugh at the prophecy once spoken about me: *The younger will rule above father and brother and his reign alone can provide his kind true sanctuary.*

Considering what was up ahead, the prophecy sounded to me like one big cosmic joke. *How could all this darkness be true sanctuary?*

Chapter 4: Aiden

I stared at the lifeless corpse of the hunter whose life Derek Novak had claimed. A wooden stake was grotesquely buried in his skull.

I wondered if I ought to tell Sofia about what had happened. Perhaps I should explain to her how the love of her life had fought against the hunters, killed one of them, then taken one of them hostage before taking their belongings and leaving them in the middle of nowhere.

We'd been following his tracks ever since. I'd given strict instructions that Derek Novak was to be kept under surveillance until he returned to The Shade. I was desperate to know the location of the island, but they'd lost him.

Incompetent fools! Of course, I kept my calm in front of my men. I'd learned long ago that my silence scared them far more than any outburst.

"Surely your daughter knows where the island is," Ivan, the

hunter whom Derek had taken hostage, suggested. "Can't we pry information out of her?"

"I believe she's been brainwashed by the vampires. She is far too in love with Derek Novak to ever give the location of the island."

"Then maybe we can reverse the effects of the brainwashing. Surely there's a way…"

"I'm not going to subject my daughter to any more damage."

He backed down just as I had expected.

My daughter seemed to hate the very sight of me. Since our confrontation, I'd placed her under lock and key. She wasn't allowed to go anywhere nor do anything without my express approval.

I kept her in a routine of training at the atrium as a new recruit, being taught how to defend herself against vampires. I expected her to keep to herself, to distance herself from the other recruits and the more trained hunters—young men and women devoted to the eradication of her beloved vampires. Thus, I was surprised to find how easy it was for her to strike up a friendship with everyone she came across with. It didn't take long for her to build a rapport with her trainers and the other recruits.

I realized what was so attractive about my daughter. She was a ray of sunshine, always accommodating and with a ready smile for those who approached her. She was beautiful and she was definitely catching the eye of several young men.

Pathetic saps. As if they could ever be deserving of my daughter… I was surprised by my own overprotectiveness.

I found it ironic that I was thinking of her in that way, considering she loathed me. In fact, when I'd first visited her at the atrium, she wouldn't even look at me. She treated me like I was invisible.

All I could do was watch her interact with the others while the director of training, Julian, updated me about her progress.

"She's learning fast," he said. "She says that Derek Novak already gave her some basic training on how to defend herself against vampires."

"Why on earth would he do that?"

"She told me that he wanted her safe. I asked her why she never used it against the vampires who attacked her and she just shrugged and told me that they were all stronger than she was, and that she's a pacifist at heart and kept forgetting to bring her wooden stake with her." There was no mistaking the hint of amusement in Julian's voice. Clearly, he was fond of my daughter. "Were you aware that she's been stabbed with one before?"

"Stabbed? By a wooden stake?"

Julian nodded. "The stake was meant for Derek Novak. She pushed him away and was stabbed instead. He fed her his blood to heal her."

The thought that she would risk her life on his behalf sickened me—the fact that she'd been drinking his blood was even worse. I hated even thinking about the things she'd been through during the period he had kept her captive at The Shade.

"What do you plan to do about that?" Julian asked.

"About what?"

"The fact that your daughter is in love with a vampire—and not just any vampire. She's in love with Derek Novak."

"I don't know." This haunted me. If I were to be honest with myself, I doubted that she was brainwashed. She didn't have the twitches, the paranoia, the confusion. She never spaced out into blank gazes. It was hard to accept, but it seemed her love for Derek Novak was genuine. *It seems that I would have to brainwash her in order to get rid of her love for that vampire.* The idea turned my stomach, and I wondered if I could really do that to my own daughter.

"She could make a great hunter."

"Trust me when I say that she is never going to be one of us." *I'm afraid she loves him too much.* I stood to my full height, squaring my shoulders as I let my gaze linger on Sofia, overcome by the emotions that coursed through me. *I made a mistake abandoning her, but how could I have kept her with me?*

"Are you all right, Reuben?"

"Give me a regular report on her progress. From now on, she is to keep a stake on her person at all times. Also, make sure that she learns how to fire a gun. I won't have her defenseless against those creatures again."

After the conversation with Julian, I found myself wandering the corridors of the headquarters, aching at all the time I had lost with Sofia. Somehow, my meandering brought me to the last place I'd thought I wanted to be: Ingrid's cell.

She was finishing up a packet of animal blood. She grinned when she saw me enter the room.

"Wow. Aiden Claremont finally pays me a visit." She tilted her head to the side, her beautiful eyes on me, her long auburn hair falling to one side. "What did I do to deserve such an honor?"

"What happened at The Oasis? Why was Sofia there?" I pulled up a chair and sat down, gearing myself up for a conversation I wasn't even sure I wanted to have.

"Why don't you ask your little princess?"

"She refuses to talk about it." I drew a breath and revealed the thought weighing on my mind. "Do you not feel even a thread of affection for her? For me?"

Ingrid's eyes softened for but a moment before the manic look returned. "I'm sure Camilla adored you and on her good days, I'm sure she also had some love for Sofia."

It hurt to hear her refer to her former self. "Camilla was the love of my life."

Ingrid scoffed. "Sure she was."

I frowned. "You don't believe me?"

"You were the love of Camilla's life, but I doubt she was yours."

I gave her a confused look. *Did I fail to show Camilla how much I adored her?*

Ingrid rolled her eyes. "It's obvious that you have no idea what to do with that little princess of yours. If you ask me, you should place a white gown on her and offer her up to the man she belongs to. Borys Maslen."

She was a stranger. Not a trace of the woman I had loved was left. "What have you done with my wife?"

A bitter smile formed on Ingrid's face. "Camilla is dead. She died the day Sofia was born." She paused and gave me a penetrating gaze that would haunt me for days after. "You were simply too blind to realize, Aiden, that your love for Sofia killed Camilla."

CHAPTER 5: SOFIA

The moment Zinnia swung the door of my suite open, I dragged myself inside and sank onto my bed. I was exhausted. Perhaps Aiden thought that if he kept me busy every second of every day, I would somehow forget Derek.

I had to find my way back to him. That was the only thing that kept me from sinking into despair. My every waking moment was filled with thoughts of how I was going to escape the hunters and return to The Shade. I went through the training and did everything I was told; I was willing to play the part of a hunter if only to gain their trust and betray it afterwards.

Perhaps it was rebellion against my father. I hated that he was acting like a father to me now, assuming that he knew what was best for me, after abandoning me for all those years. I resented Aiden Claremont for keeping me from Derek.

"You look horrible," Zinnia told me as she rummaged through

the kitchen for something to eat—right after she had made sure that the door was locked, so I couldn't escape.

"Tell me something I don't know," I said, watching her move around the small kitchen. We could've eaten at the mess hall along with the other recruits, but I'd begged her to let me return to the suite. I was in no mood to socialize and I just wanted to get back to the room that I used to share with Derek. The suite was my sanctuary, the one place in hunter territory where Derek's presence still lingered.

"Are you going to eat?" Zinnia asked as she put a pizza in the microwave.

I shook my head.

"Ben always ate up a storm after training... Do you ever think of him?"

"Sounds like him..." I smiled bitterly, recalling Ben's handsome face. I ached whenever I thought of him. "Ben was my best friend, Zinnia. At one point, I thought I was in love with him. Of course I think about him."

Zinnia raised a brow. "But not as much as you think about Novak."

I furrowed my brows, wondering what she was getting at. She'd been acting strangely the entire day. At times, it felt as if we could be friends, then she switched to treating me as if I was the most annoying creature on earth.

"What's your point, Zinnia?"

"Nothing. No point. Just an observation."

I inwardly groaned, but it seemed she wasn't done.

"You know what I don't get? Why is Claudia still alive? After what she put him through, I find it hard to believe that Ben would ever request that she be kept alive."

Claudia had put him through hell. Even I had been confused that Ben had pleaded for Claudia's life. However, I hadn't given it much thought after Ben's burial. When Derek had left, I'd forgotten about Claudia.

"Hasn't anyone asked her yet?" I asked.

"As if we can trust anything she says…"

Curiosity overcame me. Claudia had given me absolutely no reason to trust her, but I wondered if I could make an ally out of her in order to return to The Shade. I scoffed at the thought. *I'm desperate.*

"Could you ask Aiden if I could talk to her? I have questions."

Zinnia gave me a long look. I doubted that she had any trust in me at all, so I was surprised when she shrugged and said, "All right. I'll ask."

* * *

The next day, I was escorted to Claudia's cell. I barely recognized her. For the first time since I had met her, she seemed happy to see me.

She was crumpled up in a corner, her back against the wall, her knees to her chest.

"Claudia?" I half-expected her to attack me and try to turn me into a vampire again.

Instead, her eyes lit up. A smile formed on her face as if she'd just laid eyes on a long-lost friend. "Sofia!" she exclaimed as she got to her feet and embraced me.

I stiffened.

She pulled away. "Where's Derek? Are they going to allow us to leave now? We're going back to The Shade, right?"

"Derek left... I don't know what happened to him or where he is..." I found it hard to recall why I was there. Claudia's reaction had thrown me for a loop.

"Oh." She frowned. "He won't allow me to go back to The Shade, will he? He's angry that I tried to turn you... I thought that was what he wanted, but then even Ben got angry when I did it..."

So she really did try to turn me. Because she thought it was what Derek wanted. I was beyond confused. "Why did you do it, Claudia? Why did you try to turn me?"

"You and Derek deserve to be together." She nodded as if our love was some sort of epiphany to her. "I understand that now. If you were immortal like he is, then you could be together forever. Isn't that what you want, Sofia?"

Who is this person? I had no idea if it was all an act. I decided to change the subject before she could drive me crazy with longing for Derek. "Why would Ben ask that your life be spared, Claudia? He hated your guts."

Claudia's face broke into a strange smile. "You got to him, I guess, the same way you get to everyone. Back at The Oasis, he told me that if there was any person who could forgive me for everything I'd done, it would be you."

I narrowed my eyes at her. "It was you, wasn't it? You helped Ben get out of The Oasis so he could ask help from the hunters. Is that why he asked that your life be spared? But why? Why would you help him? You're in hunter territory because of it."

"I wanted to help you and Derek."

I couldn't help but scoff. "Sorry, Claudia, but I find that hard to believe."

She rolled her eyes as she ran a hand through her mass of blonde curls. I saw in her actions a trace of the old Claudia that I had known—sadistically demented—but again, her words took me aback. "Well, of course you don't believe me. After everything you know I've done, after I helped deliver you to Borys Maslen, you'd be crazy to believe me."

"You ruined my best friend, Claudia."

"Ben reminded me so much of the Duke, but he was nothing like the man who ruined me. He didn't deserve what I put him through."

Claudia actually looked genuinely remorseful. I threw my hands in the air. "You know what? I don't even care if all of this is just some sort of act. If there's any way you can help me, then I need you to do that. I need to get back to Derek, Claudia. I need to get back to The Shade."

The moment the words came out of my lips, her face once again lit up. "Yes! The Shade! I want to go back too, Sofia. You'll take me with you, won't you?" Her childlike glee blew my mind until she finally shed light on her change of character. "Yuri will take me back, won't he?"

I hadn't seen it coming, but it appeared that after hundreds of years, Claudia had finally realized that she was desperately in love with the one vampire at The Shade who could possibly hold genuine affection for her—Yuri Lazaroff.

Chapter 6: Derek

Natalie pulled her dark hair up in a messy bun. Wearing a gray university hoodie and black leggings, she looked a lot more casual at home than she normally did.

As she ran through the plans for my journey from her safe house to The Shade, I couldn't help but appreciate her as a friend. We had some history between us, Natalie and I. The centuries had changed us both, but she remained one of my dearest friends in spite of the fact that I never fully trusted her.

"I've arranged transport for you to be brought from here to a nearby shore. You'll be leaving by jet at midnight. One of The Shade's subs should be waiting on the beach to take you to The Shade."

"How on earth were you able to communicate with anyone back at The Shade?" I asked.

She smiled. "I can't tell you my trade secrets. Even you don't have that much of an influence on me, Novak."

Faded images of that beautiful young woman who'd fascinated me from the moment I'd first laid eyes on her flashed through my mind. I'd met her right after I'd escaped from our village—not long after my father had turned Lucas, Vivienne and me into vampires. I'd hated the creature I'd become and the reality of the hunter now being the hunted had just begun to sink into me.

That night my craving for human blood was especially hard to suppress. Vivienne and I had gotten separated from Gregor and Lucas after a run-in with the hunters. I knew Vivienne was starving, because so was I, but she hadn't spoken for almost a year by then, so I wasn't expecting any complaints from her.

Natalie had somehow found us as we trekked along the walls of a nearby city, not daring to enter in case we couldn't stop killing the people we met. She took us in and fed us. She was so tender, so kind, I could barely believe that she was a vampire. That night was the first time I allowed myself to entertain the idea that goodness could still be found in creatures such as us.

It was decades later before I saw her again—both of us bloodthirsty and losing touch with our humanity. Remembering her kindness greatly influenced my decision to escape it all and convince Cora to put me to sleep. After reminding her who she had been and the impact she had had on me, I liked to think that I'd had a part in making her what she was now.

"Thank you for all your help, Natalie."

She shrugged. "It's the least I can do. For old times' sake."

I heaved a sigh. "Did you ever think we'd end up this way? Vampires living centuries past our time?"

Natalie's face softened and for a moment I thought she was

going to cry, but she just laughed dryly. "That's just life, Novak. We are what we are. There's no escaping it."

No escape. Hopelessness surged within me—something visceral fighting against that idea that our kind had no escape. *How can that be our fate? That can't be it, not when there's hope for true sanctuary.*

Sofia's face flashed through my mind. I knew her role in the prophecy, the part she had to play. The distance we had between us was keenly felt. *She's my hope.*

That was when I realized that there was no possible way I could survive what was to come unless I made a conscious effort to connect to the light she had sparked in me.

I shook my head. "I'd accept in a split second that I deserve this fate, but not you, Natalie."

"Of all the vampires I've had the pleasure, or displeasure, of knowing, you've always been my favorite, Novak." She playfully placed a finger beneath my chin and lifted my head upwards. "Do you have any questions about later?"

I shook my head. "I trust you."

"Trusting me could be your undoing."

I chuckled. "I'll keep that in mind."

We shared a glass of blood before retreating to our own bedrooms to prepare for my departure. I was mostly thinking about what I was going to see upon my return to The Shade and how Sofia was doing. *I hope she understands why I left.* I drifted off into a short nap.

* * *

I was awakened by a thud outside the bedroom. Someone was with Natalie. I took great care not to make any noise as I peeked outside my bedroom door, which was slightly ajar.

"Where is Derek Novak?"

"I have no idea what you're talking about," Natalie hissed.

I swallowed hard, panic overtaking me. At first I thought that the hunters had somehow found the safe house, but these were fellow vampires.

"You're a diplomat. You're not supposed to take sides. You shouldn't have helped him. He is wanted by every vampire coven in existence—even his own."

"You can't prove that I helped Derek."

"Who else would've helped him but you?"

I had to get out of the house or risk destroying Natalie's good standing with all the other covens. I couldn't do that to her—not after everything she had done for me.

I sneaked out of the bedroom window, still careful not to make even the smallest sound, and headed to the location of the jet Natalie had arranged for me. I looked back and whispered a thank you to Natalie. *I wouldn't be able to live with myself if anything bad happened to you because of me, Natalie. Stay safe.*

A few hours later, just before the sun was about to rise, I was sitting in the submarine that would take me back to The Shade. I wanted to feel excitement about my return to the island that had been my home for centuries, but all I felt was dread. Somehow, I already knew that what I would find wouldn't be a warm welcome, but instead complete and utter chaos.

I was right.

Chapter 7: Ingrid

No matter how much I tried, I could not rid my mind of the way Aiden had looked at me after our last conversation… as if I were some sort of monster.

He's right. That's exactly what I am now. A monster. The thought gave no consolation, even though I had fooled myself into believing that I'd already reconciled myself with that truth.

I hated myself for losing Aiden. He was a man with so much love and affection to give. Certainly no other man had been able to penetrate through the walls of my heart the way he had done, yet despite all the love he had showered upon me, I was still an empty shell, haunted by my past, a past I would kill to keep hidden.

He has no idea how much of a monster I really am.

After Aiden left me in my cell, the solitude began to drive me mad. Even before becoming a vampire, I'd hated being alone and the fact that the love of my life would never look at me the same way he used to look at Camilla was driving me insane.

I stretched myself out on the small cot—one that felt coarse and rough against my skin after the Egyptian linens at The Oasis—and screamed at the top of my lungs.

A gruff, middle-aged guard showed up on the other side of the steel bars lined with UV lighting.

"Shut up!" he bellowed at me.

I gave him my sweetest smile before purring, "Make me."

"What do you want, bloodsucker?"

"Tell your boss that I want someone to talk to."

"Why on earth would I do that? All I have to do is pull one trigger and you're dead. In my opinion—one that is shared by many here—we should just kill you and that other blonde vampire."

I sat up on the cot and began stretching my arms in the air. "I'm wondering the same thing, but right now, I'm also wondering if you'll ever allow me to take a shower. It's been days. I stink."

He wrinkled his nose as he looked at me with disgust. "We received no orders regarding that, so you'll just have to bear with the living conditions you're dealt. It's better than being a corpse."

"I want someone to talk to and I want a shower. If you don't get me that, trust me when I say there are many ways I can drive you insane. You're going to wish you never became a hunter."

At this, the guard scoffed. "What could you possibly do to…"

"I think you have orders to keep me alive and unharmed. Otherwise, I'd be as you say… a corpse." I stood up and walked toward the UV-lined steel bars. I grinned when I heard Aiden talking to someone as he passed the nearby corridor. I gripped one of the bars and screamed my lungs out because of the excruciating pain in my palms.

The guard's eyes widened in shock. "You're crazy!"

Footsteps ran toward us. "What is going on?" Aiden demanded.

"She just... she gripped the bars..."

I knew I looked crazy as I stared with amusement at my burnt palms. Unless they gave me human blood, it would take hours before my skin was healed.

"Are you trying to kill yourself, Ingrid?" Aiden glared at me.

I wanted to smile at him, but I found myself strangely hurt that he called me Ingrid and not Camilla. *You've lost him, Ingrid. Accept it.* "I'm bored, Aiden... and I'm wasting away. I want a good long bath and I want someone to talk to."

"You're a prisoner here, Ingrid. Not a guest."

My response to him was simple. I gripped the bars again.

Aiden watched—his face expressionless—as I screamed in agony. Eventually, he took a step forward, his jaw twitching as he said, "Damn it, Camilla. Stop."

I let go of the bars. *Camilla.* Despite the pain, I found a reason to smile. *I haven't totally lost him after all.*

"Boss, she's insane. She's just gonna keep torturing herself," the guard said. "Perhaps we should just kill her."

Aiden shook his head, and confirmed my suspicions that he'd never really let go of Camilla when he said, "No. Give her what she's asking for."

As he walked away, I hated to admit it to myself, but I'd never really let go of him either. *I will always love him.* Even though I could try to turn the emotion off, I didn't want to.

Chapter 8: Derek

The moment I stepped out of the submarine and into the Port—the primary entry and exit point of The Shade—Cameron Hendry, one of my most trusted friends, greeted me with a curt nod and handed me a wooden stake.

"You'll need it."

I grimaced. I'd had a sense of foreboding throughout my journey back to The Shade, but I hadn't expected this.

The majority of the Elite—some of the most powerful warriors we had at The Shade—were present at the Port when I arrived. Liana, Cameron's wife, explained, "We don't know how news of your return came out. We tried to keep it within the Council, but, well, someone got wind of it and now there's a riot outside. You've got a lot of explaining to do."

A riot. Perhaps staying at hawk headquarters would've been safer.

"Maybe there's a way we can avoid the crowd." Xavier Vaughn, an old friend of ours—one I was sure had always been in love with my twin sister, Vivienne—looked distraught. Vampires didn't age, but I could swear I could see wrinkles on his face.

What has been happening? I was about to find out just how much I owed these men and women who had remained loyal to my rule for hundreds of years.

I grimaced, balling my hands into fists. "Let's face them. If they really want to go against me, then so be it." I surged toward the exit.

Liana began to object. "Derek, you have no idea what you're getting—"

Too late. I was already at the topmost step that led to the rock wall which served as the entrance to the Port. I found myself standing face to face with Felix, who'd always been more loyal to my father than to me.

Surprise was evident in his face. A hush swept through the crowd behind him.

"What's going on?" I asked him.

"They said you were coming back."

"Well, I'm back. What nonsense is this?" It looked like almost every vampire of The Shade was present. I couldn't help but wonder where the humans were. "Who's looking after the Naturals?"

"They're hiding out at The Catacombs. With the witch. They're in a lockdown."

A lockdown? I was panicking inside, but I couldn't show it. All it took was for me to show a moment of weakness and it would be the end of me.

"The human leaders organized a lockdown after Felix and his

men threatened a culling." Liana was now standing behind me.

I couldn't help but think about Corrine, the witch keeping up the protective spell that hid the island from human detection. *If she's at The Catacombs in a lockdown, how on earth is she still keeping the spell up?*

I narrowed my eyes at Felix, who was still standing in my way. "Step aside, Felix. I want a Council meeting immediately at the Great Dome."

"Not until we get our answers." Felix stood his ground.

My vision darkened and it took all my self-control not to maim him. "Step out of my way unless you want me to rip your heart out."

"Did you hear that?" Felix screamed, throwing his arms in the air. "Our beloved king wants to kill his own subject—one who has fought and bled with him many times before."

"Yes, you heard correctly. I have no idea what is going on here, but I will get to the bottom of this and whoever is responsible will answer to me. I am Derek Novak and I am still ruler of this kingdom, so unless you want bloodshed right here and right now, every single one of you who isn't part of the Elite Council will return to your homes. Now!"

The citizens of The Shade had seen me in my darkest moments. They knew what I was capable of. When darkness took over me, I could destroy a whole battalion of our best warriors. What they didn't know was that I was fighting with every fiber of my being not to let the darkness take over. *I can't afford that.*

Even as the crowd scattered, I was trying to imagine Sofia standing right beside me. I could sense her hand on my arm, keeping my temper in check.

I drew a breath. *I miss you so much, Sofia.* I could only hope she felt the same way. *I wouldn't be able to stand the idea of you hating me.* She had promised me that she would always be mine. I knew I had her heart. I hoped she knew that she had mine.

Xavier stepped out of the Port and watched as the crowd disappeared. Felix was shifting his weight from one foot to the other, obviously not knowing what to do once he lost the power of the crowd. I didn't give him the satisfaction of throwing him a glare.

Xavier blew out a whistle. "You always did have a way with crowds, Novak… It's amazing how easy it is for you to both attract and repel them."

Despite the tension, I grinned. "I can't believe you would doubt me, my friend."

"I'm sorry that we did." Xavier shrugged. "But it's been crazy here since the fall of The Oasis."

"Let's discuss it at the Dome. It seems we have a lot of issues to take into consideration." I looked Cameron and Liana's way. "Could you make sure that Corrine and the human leaders are informed that I have returned? I want them present at the Council meeting."

This is just the calm before the storm, Derek. Don't fool yourself into believing that things are about to get better.

At that moment, the only refuge from the turmoil inside of me was the image of my beautiful Sofia—her smile, her eyes, her laugh.

What have you done, Derek? What made you think you could get through all of this without her? What are you going to do now?

Hopelessness began to overtake me as I saw the island I fought for—my kingdom—for what it was: a place absolutely devoid of light.

Chapter 9: Ingrid

The hunters resented that I was ordering them around. I could hear them murmuring amongst themselves. Not only had Aiden allowed me to have a shower and a companion, he'd moved not only me but also the impetuous blonde vampire to our very own quarters.

The bedroom reminded me of my dorm room in college. Two beds, closets, a shared bathroom... It wasn't the kind of space I was used to having, but it was better than the cell.

The moment I was brought to the room, I noticed the sealed windows. *Definitely no sunlight coming in through those...* Surveillance cameras watched our every move. I was certain that the room was bugged so they could hear our every conversation.

I didn't care. I grabbed a towel from a closet and stripped to my underwear, winking at whoever was watching me through the cameras.

I stepped into the bathroom and took a long bath. By the time I stepped out, Claudia was already seated on one of the beds, a blank expression on her face.

I wasn't pleased about spending time with the little twerp, but I guessed she had to do. I fought the urge to roll my eyes at the petty conversations I'd have to endure with her.

I got dressed, not caring who saw me naked, before taking a seat on the bed across from hers. I perused her form as I towel-dried my hair. I could tell that she hadn't been given any favors when it came to personal hygiene either.

"Aren't you going to have a bath?" I asked.

"Maybe later." She stared at me.

"What?" I snapped at her.

"You're Ingrid Maslen. Sofia's mother."

I frowned. "What if I am?"

"I hope Sofia gets to escape this place. She really wants to, I think. She and Derek are so in love." Her gaze left me as she bowed her head. "I hope she takes me with her. I want to go back to The Shade. Yuri is back there."

The news about Sofia's escape was delightful, but I knew that asking further would draw suspicion. Claudia went on with her own soliloquy. "Have you ever felt like you're unworthy of the love of a man?"

Yes.

"He's done everything for you and yet none of it seems to be enough."

My life's story.

"I've always felt that way about Yuri. He always came through for me. And all I did was hurt him, betray him, and make a fool out of him for holding any affection toward a broken creature like me."

Broken creature. The words struck such a chord with me that I couldn't pry my eyes away from Claudia.

"Then you lose him," Claudia continued, her gaze distant, her eyes moistening. "You mess up so bad, you feel as if nothing you do could ever get him back. You start to wonder if he could ever forgive you, if he could ever love you again, but all the while, you know you don't deserve that love…"

She paused and I found myself finishing her sentence. "You don't deserve it, but it doesn't mean you don't want it."

Claudia nodded. "Exactly. How did you know?"

"I feel the same way about someone." The truth hurt. *I'm in love with Aiden. I always will be. There's no escaping it, but it doesn't mean that I have to be prisoner to that love.* "Claudia, if you had the chance, would you try to go back to him and make up for everything? If he welcomed you with open arms…"

Her face lit up. "Yes! I would do anything. I've been such a fool…"

Claudia wanted love more than she wanted power. I, on the other hand, had chosen power over love a long time ago. I stared at Claudia—someone strong and capable, turned into a weakling by love. *I refuse to be like her. I can't be the way Camilla was—a whimpering housewife, lovesick over her husband. I'm Ingrid Maslen now. Camilla Claremont is long gone.*

I looked at the room I was in, a favor I didn't deserve—proof that Aiden still held affection for me. Should I choose Claudia's path, I knew I could get him back, but I also shuddered at the thought. Camilla was in love with Aiden. Not Ingrid.

If I'm to be Ingrid Maslen, then Aiden is my greatest weakness. I swallowed hard. *That only means one thing… He must be destroyed.*

Chapter 10: Sofia

No matter how tired I was, there were nights when sleep eluded me. Moments spent with Derek haunted me. *Is he safe at The Shade? If he is, why hasn't he tried to get me back? Is he even thinking about me?*

Sometimes, I'd get so overwhelmed with the questions, I could barely breathe. I would hold the diamond pendant he gave me for my birthday, thumbing its edges, drawing comfort from the promise that came with it: *"I want you to have it. Wear it always. It will remind you of me. Take it as a promise from me—a promise that I will find a way to be with you."*

I didn't know where he was or if he was in danger. I couldn't understand why he'd thought it best to leave without even saying goodbye, but I was sure of one thing… I could never doubt his love for me. That was the hope that carried me to the next day.

Aside from Derek, one more thing bothered my every waking

moment: *I am the immune.* It was one thing I didn't know how to find the answers to. Telling the hunters about it didn't seem like the best idea, considering how I had no clue how they would react to me revealing that I should've been turned into a vampire many times, but here I was—human still.

Only one other person at hunter headquarters knew that I was immune: Ingrid. The thought of speaking to her made me shudder. I came to the point of desperation, however, and asked my father to let me speak to her.

"Why on earth would you want to talk to that woman? The same woman who gave you as a gift to Borys Maslen, and still wants to even now?"

"I want to speak with her. In private. No bugs." I'd been at headquarters long enough to know that it was difficult to have any conversation in private.

"You can't trust a word that comes out of her mouth, Sofia."

At that, I couldn't help but scoff. "You mean the same way I can't trust a word that comes out of yours?"

He seemed genuinely offended. "Why is it so hard for you to believe that I'm on your side? I'm keeping you here for your own safety. I'm your father."

"You say that like it means something. You're my father by blood. So what? You abandoned me with the Hudsons for nine years, Aiden! Camilla offered me up as a sacrifice to Borys Maslen and she's my mother!"

Aiden stood up, gripping the edge of his desk so tightly his knuckles turned white. "I am nothing like Ingrid. I didn't want you involved in all this. I wanted you to have a normal life... Something I was deprived of because of the double life I had to live as both a hunter and a businessman."

I wasn't in the mood to discuss his shortcomings as a father. "It doesn't matter. The past is the past. We can't change it. For now, do you really want to gain my trust?"

He sat back in his seat. "I would do anything to gain your trust, Sofia."

I raised a brow. "Anything? How about you take me to Derek."

"I can't do that and you know it. Even if I could, I wouldn't know how to find him. I don't know where Novak is. He might be at The Shade, but I doubt you'd trust me with that information."

"Well, if you can't take me to Derek, then take me to Ingrid. Let me talk to her."

Aiden gave me a look of concern, as if he was afraid of what Ingrid could say to me. I realized then that he was trying to protect me from getting hurt. For the first time, I appreciated what it felt like to have a father looking after me. I thought it sad that it had taken him a decade to make me feel that way. I missed him so much, but it felt like any affection he showed me came too late. At this point, I detested how he was butting into my life. Still, I truly hoped that he had my best interest in heart—now and in the past.

"I was never able to control Camilla," Aiden revealed wistfully. "She had a mind of her own and she was given to mood swings when we were together. I guess I won't be able to control you either, will I?"

"You can try, but I think that question is rhetorical."

"Very well then… I'll take you to your mother."

Suddenly I remembered all that I had gone through at The

Oasis. *Borys's claws sinking into my thighs, his teeth biting into my neck, his hands groping my body…* All the while my mother had sat back, doing nothing,

I swallowed hard. Any sense of anticipation I felt about meeting Ingrid was replaced with pure dread. *What exactly am I getting myself into?*

CHAPTER 11: DEREK

The Great Dome was the center of all our governmental, judicial and military gatherings. It never failed to remind me of my twin sister, Vivienne, to whom I'd given the task of modernizing the Dome.

At that moment, the wave of nostalgia and grief that came with my sister's passing away at the hands of the hunters wasn't the only reason I was hesitant to go to the Dome. The Elite Council was already waiting there. I was going to face opposition. Truth be told, that wasn't what I was afraid of. Instead, I was afraid of myself.

Neither Sofia nor Vivienne were there to reel me in. Neither of them would be there to remind me that I was capable of goodness.

Still, when Ashley and Sam, two of Sofia's closest friends at The Shade, showed up at my penthouse to let me know that Liana had instructed them to escort me to the Dome, I had no choice but to go.

Thus, I found myself walking along the torchlit corridors of the Crimson Fortress and climbing the west tower, which stood as high as one hundred and fifty feet. Roofed with pointed cross-arches, the tower was one of the first parts built in the fortress and had already witnessed many battles in defense of the island. The Crimson Fortress lined the entire island with thick walls and fortified towers.

"What happened, Derek? Where's Sofia?" Ashley was the youngest vampire at The Shade. She had been one of the human teenagers brought for my harem—a sick tradition that had somehow developed at The Shade during my four-hundred-year sleep. It involved the abduction of teenagers from outside the island to be brought to the Elite as slaves. Among the girls who had been brought with Ashley had been Sofia and Rosa. Ashley was the only one who had chosen to be turned into one of us. Still, despite the fact that she was one of my subjects, she never acknowledged me as royalty, but always spoke to me as she would a friend—something I liked about her.

"You'll find out soon enough," I answered as I caught sight of the entrance to the Dome right ahead of us. I gave Ashley a look before diverting my attention to Sam. "What's been going on here?"

The two exchanged glances and I immediately concluded that they were no longer just friends. *At least there's still some good news here.* I was aware of Ashley's affection toward Sam after she had blurted out the whole thing to me back at Sofia's quarters at The Catacombs.

I gave them a knowing nod. Whatever joy I felt for my friends was quickly swept away, however, as I stepped in front of the giant double oak doors of the Dome.

A commotion had obviously been happening right before my arrival, but the moment I stepped in, a chilly silence filled the hall. I sped my way toward my seat at the front of the hall.

Eli Lazaroff, who presided over all of our Council meetings, took his place at the stand, in the middle of the Dome. He cleared his throat as he faced me. "Your highness…" He bowed his head and shuffled his feet. I could tell that he was unsure how to bring up all the issues that had been brewing at The Shade since I had left to rescue Sofia.

"Oh, for crying out loud…" Felix stood and began walking toward the stand. "May I please take the stand?"

I inwardly groaned as I gave him a nod. Eli left the stand to give Felix the platform he was demanding.

"With all due respect, Derek, I need to be straight with you," Felix began. "You are savior of The Shade—none of us can take that away from you. We bled with you and fought alongside you, but how can we continue to serve under your rule when we are uncertain of your loyalties not only toward this kingdom, but to all vampires in general?"

I narrowed my eyes at him. "You're questioning my loyalty? Do you not remember the prophecy and how I am to bring our kind true sanctuary? How could I turn my back on vampires when my life's purpose is to save us?"

"I can't believe that you will remain true to this prophecy. Not after you were instrumental in the ruin of The Oasis and the Maslens. Not after you stepped into hunter territory and came out without a scratch. Did you or did you not work with the hunters to destroy The Oasis in order to rescue the woman you love?"

It felt like I was being tried for a crime I had not committed—by a subordinate of mine at that. I straightened in my seat, swallowing back my rising temper, shutting my eyes for a moment to remember who I was when I was with Sofia. I gripped my seat's armrests as I struggled to push away the darkness overtaking me.

"I did not work with the hunters to take down The Oasis. At the time of their attack, I was being held prisoner by Borys Maslen. I was in chains, being tortured. If it weren't for Sofia, I never would've made it out of there." I deliberately left out the fact that my brother, Lucas, had been there. He'd died during the hunter attack on The Oasis, and despite his hatred toward me, part of me grieved his loss. "Use your common sense. Why on earth would the hunters ever work with me?"

"Why else would they treat you as a guest in their territory and let you prance out of there alive?" Felix shrugged. "Isn't it because your beloved Sofia is the daughter of the notorious leader of the hunters, Reuben?"

"How do you even know of all of this, Felix?"

A hush filled the Dome when the doors swung open and a prominent figure at The Shade stepped inside.

My father had a flair for the dramatic, but I never could've predicted that he'd be back in The Shade before me, and from the reactions of my allies, it seemed they hadn't been aware either.

Gregor Novak took his place beside Felix at the stand. "I told him everything, son. It's your word against mine now."

"You know that I never worked with the hunters."

My father shook his head. "I'm not so sure about that. You've elevated the standing of every human of The Shade. You left the island to save one human girl from the Maslens. You stayed with the hunters for weeks. I think we deserve answers."

Just like that, reality sank in—not only to me, but to everyone present there.

The king of The Shade was now on trial.

CHAPTER 12: SOFIA

Upon my request, Aiden agreed to have Ingrid brought to my suite. I felt safer on my own turf, and it seemed Aiden felt better too.

"You summoned me?" Ingrid said.

I got straight to the point. "Why am I immune? What does being 'the immune' mean?"

She smiled with what almost seemed like affection. "I don't know, Sofia. You should be a Maslen, a beautiful nine-year-old vampire, but you're not. All I know is that since the moment he tasted your blood, Borys has been obsessed with you."

"Why? What's in my blood?"

"I'm curious myself. Perhaps you should let me have a taste so that I could find out for myself?... I'm sorry. Bad joke." A moment of silence ensued as she eyed me with what looked like longing. "You must have so many questions. How have you been,

Sofia? I've been hearing whispers about Derek disappearing…"

A lump formed in my throat at the mention of Derek. I wasn't sure I wanted to talk to Ingrid—or anyone else for that matter—about him. I ached with longing at the very mention of his name.

"You miss him, don't you? I understand how you feel."

"Why?" I asked, unable to hide the resentment in my voice. "Because it's the same way you feel about your beloved Borys right now?"

The question sparked anger in her eyes, but she shook her head. "No. It's what I felt about your father during my first years at The Oasis. It felt like I was missing a part of me."

"We're not the same. I didn't leave Derek. I'm fighting to get back to him."

"Forget Derek, Sofia."

That's impossible. I knew how obsessed my mother was about giving me to Borys. Harping on about Derek wasn't going to help my situation. "Is that what you did with Aiden? You forgot him?"

"It can be done, you know. Is it true that you're married to Derek? Or were you bluffing?"

"I'm engaged to him, but no, we're not married."

Relief washed over her face. "Claudia told me that you wanted to escape in order to get back to Derek. Is this true?"

I pursed my lips, fighting the urge to roll my eyes. *What has happened to Claudia?* She'd been useless in finding a way out of headquarters. The only reaction from her was how much she wanted to get back to The Shade and whether Yuri would even care. *It's like all common sense left her the moment she left The Shade.* I couldn't help but smile a bit. *I guess that's what love can do to a person.*

"If it is?"

"I want to help you."

I raised a brow, taken by surprise. "Why?"

"I want you out of here. As long as you're here, Borys can't get to you."

"So what you're saying is that you want me out of headquarters so that Borys can abduct me?"

"It sounds wicked when you put it that way."

"You're my mother. Does that not mean anything to you?"

"It means everything to me, Sofia. Trust me when I say that if it weren't for you, Ingrid Maslen would probably not exist."

I had no idea what she was talking about. I wasn't sure I wanted to know. "How do you propose to help me?"

"Easy. All I have to do is pretend to be Camilla Claremont again."

She sounded like a lunatic. How on earth had I ended up with such demented parents? The thought of ever becoming like them horrified me.

She stood up. "If you're agreeing to let me help you, get up and embrace me. Now," she instructed.

I didn't know what came over me, but I complied, hugging my mother for the first time in a decade.

"The only reason I want you to be with Borys is because I want what's best for you," she whispered into my ear. "If you're with him, you won't become like Camilla was. With Derek, you'll be a weakling. With Borys, you'll become strong."

I was trembling and I began fighting back the tears when she kissed me on the cheek. When we broke our embrace, I realized why she had asked for it in the first place.

Aiden had just walked in the room—in time to see what appeared to be a poignant moment between mother and daughter.

Feeling used, I looked from Aiden to Ingrid and was surprised to find her wiping away tears as she took my hand in hers and squeezed tight. "I know how hard it is for you to believe, but I love you, Sofia."

I smiled at her, knowing that no matter how much I wanted to believe her declaration, it was a bald-faced lie.

Chapter 13: Aiden

"What game are you playing, Ingrid?"

She stopped on the way back to her room and faced me. "What game?"

"Don't play coy with me, Ingrid. The last time we spoke, you made it clear that you hold no affection for our daughter. Now I step into her suite and you're all hugs and kisses with her? What's your game?"

"I just had a heart-to-heart with my daughter, Aiden. Is it so impossible that I could have a change of heart toward her?"

"A change of heart? After you fed her to Borys Maslen? Did you see it happen? Did you watch as he bit into her? Did you like seeing him hurt her? Did you not feel any guilt at the sight?" I began stepping toward her, backing her up until her back hit one of the walls. "What is wrong with you? Sofia is your daughter. How could that not mean anything to you?"

She raised a brow and scoffed. "It meant nothing to my mother that I was her daughter."

There it was again—another clue about a past she refused to talk about. During the first years of our marriage, I'd encouraged her to seek professional help. She'd never even entertained my suggestion. I had to watch the woman I loved remain broken, with no hope of ever getting fixed.

I became keenly aware of her closeness. The longing I'd had for her flooded me. Whether she was Ingrid or Camilla, she still had the same effect on me now as she had done when I had first laid eyes on her. She left me breathless. She drew me in like no other woman had ever done before. No matter how much I hated to admit it, I would always love Camilla.

Before I could stop myself, I grabbed her by the shoulders and pressed my lips against hers.

She's not Camilla. She's Ingrid. She's a vampire, a monster, a creature you're sworn to rid this planet of. You're in hawk headquarters. Think of what you stand to lose should you be seen. None of it mattered. I pushed against her with all the strength in me, claiming what I'd been deprived of since she'd left me—her touch, her kiss, her form uniquely contoured to fit mine.

She responded with abandon. It wasn't until her fangs cut my lower lip that I jerked away from her. We were both stunned as I wiped the trace of blood from my lip.

"You still love me, don't you?" She spoke wistfully.

"I think I always will," I admitted, hating myself. "Don't think for one moment, Ingrid, that my love for Camilla erases the fact that you're using my daughter for whatever sick things you've got planned. If you ever hurt Sofia again, make no mistake about it, I will kill you myself."

Her eyes began to brim with tears as she nodded. "I understand. I just… I don't know how to be a good mother, Aiden. I want to be that for her, but I don't know how. I want to change. I want to make amends with her, even if only to get back in your good graces, because I love you, Aiden. I will always love you."

I couldn't tell if it was genuine or if she was just putting on an act. At that point, I couldn't think straight enough to care if it was true.

I was fully aware of the consequences when I took her to my suite and made love to her, but I didn't care. I held her in my arms and gave in to my desperate need for the woman I had loved, to fill the emptiness that she had left inside me when she had abandoned me and our daughter.

That night, like so many others before her disappearance, I found that I was once again putty in the hands of Camilla Claremont.

It wasn't until the morning after, waking up with her lovely form cradled in my arms, that it sank in that Camilla was long gone and that it was Ingrid Maslen who now held my deepest affections in the palm of her hand.

Aiden, what have you done?

Chapter 14: Gregor

Upon my return to The Shade, only one word could describe me: haunted. Every part of me wished that I had never left the island—never gone along with Lucas' plan to take Sofia to The Oasis.

I'd known that I had made a mistake the moment I had stepped into the Maslens' infamous Egyptian tombs. The Shade was my kingdom and I never should've left it. Now, after the destruction of The Oasis and the fall of the Maslens, things would never again be the same.

I shuddered whenever I thought about everything that had happened since my son, Derek, had woken up from his four-hundred-year sleep. I'd never thought that I could feel as much hatred and resentment toward my own flesh and blood as I had felt for Derek when he had taken over The Shade and dethroned me as king of the island. Now, back at the island, I had no choice but to ruin him.

I wanted my throne back. No matter what those fools belonging to the Elite thought, I was the rightful ruler of The Shade. Derek never should've taken that place from me.

Standing in the middle of the Dome, I could feel my blood boiling as I stared at my son, sitting where I should've been seated. I would go as far as declaring war on him if it meant regaining my rightful place.

"Ever since that little vixen of yours arrived at The Shade, you've turned this kingdom upside down on her behalf." I relished how Derek's face tensed. Never before had something like this happened at The Shade. When I'd been king, my subjects had never had reason to doubt my loyalty. Now that doubt was being cast on Derek, I had every intention of capitalizing on it.

"Sofia has nothing to do with the choices I made regarding The Shade."

"Isn't she the reason you stopped the culling and asked Eli to organize a way to tap into the blood banks? This move puts The Shade in danger of being discovered, does it not?"

"The same way you put The Shade in danger when you started abducting teenagers to turn into your slaves. Only with this measure, we don't have to destroy any lives." Derek was losing patience and it was obvious.

I smiled inwardly. I wanted his temper to blow up. I wanted to see him make a fool of himself.

I had once again underestimated my son. Before I could think of another accusation, he stood up and scoped out the round hall.

"I tire of this. I am still ruler of this kingdom and will not be subjected to this mock trial. I am loyal to The Shade and will remain loyal to it. I am prophesied to find our kind true sanctuary and I will do that until I am robbed of my immortality. My love for Sofia Claremont is no secret to any of you. She is prophesied to be instrumental in helping me fulfill the prophecy. I am not working with the hunters. Yes, I stayed in hunter territory after the fall of The Oasis until my return here. Sofia Claremont is the daughter of one of the highest-ranking hunters in the world and he let me go because I agreed to never see her again."

At that, many of those present began to react.

"Does this mean that Sofia's not going to return to the island?"

"Are you really going to stay away from her?"

"What about the prophecy? If you're apart from Sofia you may never be able to bring our kind true sanctuary."

"How did you ever get Sofia to agree to let you leave?"

"Does Sofia know that her father struck that bargain with you?"

"How could you have ever agreed?"

The questions were irrelevant. Angry that I could be sidelined so easily, I surged forward, letting out a scream. I attacked Derek, managing to claw his cheek before he could dodge me.

His blue eyes shifted to me as the wound healed.

"You have no idea what you're up against," I warned him, even as I shut out from my memory the events that had occurred between the time Borys Maslen and I had escaped The Oasis up to the time I'd been released to return to The Shade. I could feel the darkness taking over me.

"What exactly am I up against, Father? You?"

"You never should've gone against me."

"Empty threats, Father. We both know you have no power here."

Derek was underestimating me. I wasn't the same man who'd left The Shade for The Oasis. No, not anymore. "This is war, Derek."

He stood to his full height and squared his shoulders. "Then so be it, Father. If it's war you want, it's war you're going to get."

We stared each other down, ignoring the commotion surrounding us. At that moment, Derek and I had an understanding. As long as the war went on, I was no longer his father and he was no longer my son.

You have no idea what you've just gotten yourself into, I thought as I walked away from the Dome. *I've changed the same way Borys has changed. I shudder to think of what kind of a force Borys is now. Derek doesn't stand a chance against us. He picked the wrong side when he chose light over darkness.*

As I left the Crimson Fortress, the smile faded from my face when an image of Sofia Claremont flashed through my mind along with the command: *She must be destroyed if Derek is to come back as a child of the darkness.*

I realized then why I loathed the lovely redhead so much.

She was Derek's choice. She was the light that he'd chosen over the darkness.

Chapter 15: Derek

"What is going on here?" I demanded the moment I saw Corrine at The Catacombs.

After finally escaping the confrontation at the Dome, I'd sought out the witch who was crucial to the ongoing survival of The Shade. Of all the human leaders established by Sofia to represent the human population of The Shade, only Gavin and Ian showed up to meet me. They explained to me that Corrine was still at The Catacombs; thus, I was forced to visit the network of caves located in a vast mountain range at the northernmost part of the island known as the Black Heights.

Corrine was seated at the living room of the quarters that I had prepared for Sofia when she had moved to live with the other humans at The Catacombs. The witch barely even batted an eyelash at the sight of me. "You're here."

"This island is going to fall apart unless we all do the work necessary for its survival." I'd lost my patience back at the Dome. "Why are you supporting this lockdown?"

"I'm not supporting it." She shook her head. "I'm just here to make sure these people don't end up killing each other. Do you have any idea how chaotic it's been in your kingdom since you disappeared?"

My jaw tightened. "I've been told."

"Where is Sofia?"

"I left her with the hunters."

"You're up against more than you can handle here, Derek. You just declared civil war within The Shade. The Naturals are at one another's throats… Never before has The Catacombs experienced such a high crime rate. And if I'm not mistaken, there are also rumors of an attack from covens outside The Shade. It's anarchy and war all at the same time."

"Well, thank you for giving me such a wonderful recap." I was thankful for the privacy given us by the humans and vampires who had accompanied me to The Catacombs, because if there was anybody at The Shade I felt safe losing my temper with, it was Corrine. She could easily placate me with a single spell.

"You never should've left Sofia. You are weakest when you are apart from her."

"I didn't have a choice. Keeping her with me would've destroyed her. Even now, whenever I think of her—just the image of her in my mind—it makes me crave her blood so much. All I can think about is how good it felt to drink her blood."

Corrine's eyes grew wide. "You've tasted Sofia's blood? How? Why?"

The recollection made me swallow hard. "She fed me her blood to save me. Borys had been torturing me. We needed to escape The Oasis. I tried to object, but Sofia insisted. She cut her wrist and let the blood drip into my mouth... I healed quicker than ever before."

Corrine sat up straight and moved to the edge of the couch. "That's it? Never again did you..."

I shook my head. "I craved her so much after... She willingly let me drink from her neck when we were in hunter territory."

"Derek, how could you..."

"Don't." I shook my head. "I do enough beating myself up. I don't need you to add to my guilt."

She remained pensive for a couple of seconds. "What did it feel like to have her blood running inside of you?"

"Honestly? It made me feel powerful beyond measure."

Corrine stared at me, the expression on her face impossible to decipher. She opened her mouth to say something, but then Rosa entered the room. Her eyes widened with surprise.

"Derek! I had no idea you were back..."

Rosa reddened, almost as if she'd been caught doing something she ought not to do.

I squinted at her and frowned. "You don't seem very happy to see me, Rosa. Is something wrong?"

With everything going on, I was pleased to see Rosa. Always careful around me, she reminded me of the days back at my penthouse when she, Ashley and Sofia had lived with me. I felt a sense of responsibility toward her and I found myself eager to know how she'd been doing since I had left.

Rosa stood still as she tried to figure out if I was upset with her. Corrine rolled her eyes. "You're scaring her, Derek."

I chuckled and the girl sighed with relief. "How have you been, Rosa?"

She blushed and nodded. "I'm fine."

"Rosa's been taking care of Sofia's quarters," Corrine explained. "We didn't know what to expect, but it's been overcrowded here at The Catacombs lately, so I recommended that they move here."

My brow quirked up. "Who are *they* exactly?"

"Well, Rosa's been here all along, but now so is Gavin and his family—Lily and the children. Ian and Anna have moved in too."

Gavin and Ian were both Naturals—born and raised at The Shade. When Sofia had moved to The Catacombs, it was Gavin who had taken her under his wing and introduced her to life within the caves. Lily was his mother and he had two younger siblings, Rob and Madeline. At some point, Gavin had introduced Sofia to Ian, who had been at the time one of the rebel leaders at The Shade. Together, the three of them had spearheaded a protest against a culling of humans deemed to be useless.

"Who's Anna?" I asked, not familiar with the name.

Corrine and Rosa exchanged uncomfortable glances. Rosa took a seat on a wooden chair near her as if to grab support for what Corrine was about to reveal.

"Anna was a Migrate. She was Felix's slave. For a time, it seemed that he was actually in love with her. He had everyone convinced, but eventually he tired of her and abandoned her here at The Catacombs. We don't know what happened between them, but she went insane…"

"So you have a crazy woman living in Sofia's quarters?" I frowned.

Corrine glared at my nonchalance. I found the story

heartbreaking, but it was standard fare at The Shade. Anna was lucky that Felix had kept her alive. I wasn't glad that she'd gone crazy, but what was I to do?

Rosa was quick to explain. "Well, you see, Gavin and Ian already suspected that some of the men here at The Catacombs were"—she paused and swallowed hard—"taking advantage of Anna. I'm not sure about the details, but Ian and Kyle got into a fight with some of the older Naturals over her. Since then, both of them have had this weird rivalry over who gets to protect her. That's why Ian insisted that he move here with Anna, something Kyle's not very happy about."

Kyle was one of two guards I trusted. He and Sam weren't part of the Elite families who'd fought with me in order to establish The Shade. They'd moved to the island much later, seeking The Shade's refuge against the relentless pursuit by the hunters. They'd proven loyal and worthy of my trust. They were also good friends with Sofia.

Sofia. It felt like I was surrounded by her. These people were her friends. The Catacombs was her world. I was sitting inside her home. I was suddenly so aware of her absence, it caused a heavy weight to settle on my chest.

Corrine stared directly at me. "You're out of your depth, Novak. Get Sofia back here. There's no other way."

Chapter 16: Ingrid

The morning after Aiden and I made love, he found me cowering in a corner from the sunlight streaming through his large bedroom windows. I could swear he snickered when he saw me. I couldn't help but shoot him a look of thankfulness when he pulled the heavy drapes shut.

He pulled a robe over his body before turning to look at me. "No one can know this happened."

That hurt. I wondered if he had even the slightest clue what it did to me when he took me in his arms and held me like he had before—like I was Camilla. It felt like forgiveness, like redemption, like acceptance.

You're such a fool, Ingrid. He used you. That's what he did.

He began gathering my clothes and placed them on the bed. "Get dressed." He walked to the bathroom. Minutes later, the shower started running.

My knees were still shaking as I stood. I wasn't sure if it was because of the sunlight or the reality of what had just happened. I'd never enjoyed sharing the marriage bed all those years. I'd tried my best to please him, because I loved him, but to me, it was my duty as his wife and not something I relished.

This time, I'd given in to him with abandon. Perhaps it was the time and the distance that had kept us apart for the best part of a decade. I wasn't sure why, but I'd wanted him as much as I felt he wanted me. I'd given myself to him without inhibition.

Is it because I was with him as Ingrid and not as Camilla?

I didn't have time to process all the emotions. I'd barely finished slapping my clothes on when he stepped out of the shower, dripping wet, a robe over his muscular form.

He stared at me. I would've given anything to be able to read his mind at that moment. His face was blank.

My heart broke when he said, "Let's go. You can wash up back in your room."

That was it. Aiden thought that everything that had happened between us was one big mistake, a lapse of judgment on his part. I was certain that it would be the last time.

Thus, I was surprised when, in the middle of the night, he arrived in the bedroom I shared with Claudia, bringing our nightly ration of animal blood. He handed both Claudia and me our respective containers before shuffling his feet. I took my container and stared up at him, wondering why he wouldn't leave. After what had happened, I wasn't very thrilled to have him around and, strange as it was, the idea of drinking blood in front of him felt wrong.

"I need to speak with you."

"Let's speak then." I placed the container on my bedside table.

"You're not going to drink that?"

I shook my head. "I'm not that hungry…"

"Very well." Aiden nodded for me to follow him. I followed him out of the bedroom, not knowing what to expect.

He took me to the elevator and we were soon headed for the basement. I took note of where we were passing through. Nobody was around. No guards, no other people at all. Just us. It wasn't long after when we walked through a network of secret passages under the headquarters. Eventually, we reached a short flight of stairs that led up to a latched opening. Aiden pushed it open and we stepped into a garden I assumed was somewhere south of the main estate. Headquarters was a long walk away from us.

The moment I stepped out of the underground passages, Aiden took one long, yearning look at me before grabbing me by the waist and kissing me.

For a moment, I was too stunned to react. After I gathered my wits about me, I responded with abandon.

I realized that night that I had him. I had Aiden Claremont in the palm of my hand.

I also discovered a way to destroy Sofia—and perhaps, in the process, destroy Aiden and any love I still felt for him.

The sense of power I felt that night, knowing that everything seemed to be falling into place, was unlike anything I had felt before. Snuggling into his arms and looking up at his beautiful green eyes, I smiled up at Aiden and he smiled back.

"I don't think I could ever stop loving you," he admitted.

My heart leapt. "Nor I you, Aiden."

That's exactly why I need to ruin you. Just imagine how powerful I'll be once I no longer have love holding me back.

CHAPTER 17: CLAUDIA

I couldn't keep Yuri out of my mind—not since I'd left The Shade. He was the one constant in my life. Ever since the first day I had met him, he had always been part of my life—until I'd become stupid enough to leave.

I pushed back the tears as memories came to mind of the first day I met him.

Once every week, my master, the Duke, would send me to market. That day was my favorite, because it meant I could take the long walk past the woods to town, away from the horrors of the Duke's manor.

I was his favorite. He never shared me with anyone else, but being the Duke's favorite was not something to be envied. From the moment I'd been brought to him, I was pitied by everyone in the manor. I even pitied myself, and I hated that.

As I walked past the woods that would lead me to town, I wondered why I hadn't yet resigned myself to this fate.

That afternoon, I found out why. That was the afternoon I met Yuri for the first time.

He popped out of nowhere. I figured he had been by the nearby brook and saw me walking along the lonesome path. So he began walking in stride with me.

"Hello. I'm Yuri," he said, flashing me a smile, his hands clasped behind his back. "Might I have the honor of knowing your name, miss?"

I didn't trust men and he was no exception. I slipped one hand into a hidden pocket in my dress where I kept a dagger. I was willing to use it on him if I had to.

"So you're not going to give me your name, huh? That's fine. Are you off to town? That's where I'm headed too. Mind if I walk with you?"

I remained silent. I couldn't deny, however, how attractive I found him. He was at least six inches taller than me, with a lean build and a dimple that appeared whenever he smiled. His nose was slightly crooked in a way that added to his charm. He had a boyishness about him that drew me in. He was nothing like the Duke at all. Many would say that the Duke was far more handsome than Yuri. Many women thought the Duke was the perfect specimen of a man.

I knew better. The Duke caused me nothing but pain.

I was so busy studying Yuri's features and losing myself in melancholic thoughts of how powerless I was against the Duke that I barely noticed Yuri was still waiting for a response from me. When he didn't get an answer, he just kept walking beside me.

"We just moved into the village recently. Me and my older brother, Eli. He got work as a tutor for the Maslens. He's really smart and he wants to be an inventor someday. I think he can do it. I wasn't

pleased about moving here with him, but I figured this place is as good as any to hone my art. When we got here, I was so disappointed... that is, until I saw you last week. I was hoping you'd allow me to paint you."

For some reason, I wanted to say yes, but being around Yuri would get me in trouble with the Duke, so once again, I just kept silent. Again, he didn't seem to mind. Apart from me shaking my head when he asked me if I was deaf or mute or maybe both, I didn't respond to his talk. He talked on anyway.

That was the way it was every week. He would show up and tell me about his week, how he and his brother were doing, what new art project he was out to do, which new friends he had made. I would often try to hide a smirk or a scowl whenever he would mention a name that I would recognize—a face I'd already seen at the Duke's brothel. Still, I never talked to him. I kept silent, and satisfied myself with listening to him.

I hadn't realized the effect Yuri had had on me until one day when the Duke questioned me about why I always had a smile on my face after returning from the market. I told him that I enjoyed the long walks.

"Liar!" He backhanded me so powerfully that I fell to the ground. "Don't you dare lie to me, Claudia. Ever!"

He put me through hell that night. It didn't end until I was bloody and bruised all over. I couldn't walk for days and once I was able to get up, every step still caused me pain.

The Duke didn't need to tell me. I just knew. I was to stay away from Yuri for my own good.

For two weeks, I wasn't able to go to the market. The Duke sent someone else instead. When he decided that I was ready to go, he warned me, "Walk alone, Claudia. You must always walk alone from now on."

That afternoon, as I started my trek toward town, Yuri once again appeared. I could see the delight in his eyes upon seeing me. It made what I had to do even more difficult. The moment he began walking beside me, I stopped and turned toward him.

"Please stop. I would much prefer walking alone from now on. Thank you very much."

"Did I do something wrong?" he asked. "It's the first time I've ever heard your voice, and you use it to make me go away. It's a lovely voice. I hope it comes with a name."

"Please. It's best that you stay away from me."

I knew that he could sense something was wrong, but he just nodded. "I understand."

I wondered what it was that he understood. Did he think that I didn't desire his company? I longed for it every week.

He handed me a piece of paper. "You didn't show up the past two weeks, so I figured something went wrong or maybe you got tired of me. Whatever your reason is, I want you to have this. I told you I would paint you. I hope you like it."

I simply stared at it, not knowing whether to take it.

"Please take it. It's not much, but, well… it's my birthday today. I would really appreciate it if you took this small token of my affection."

I didn't know how to resist. I was trembling as I took the folded piece of canvas. It's his birthday today. That means he's twenty-one. Older than me, but a lot younger than the Duke.

I opened the paper and drew a breath. It was a painting of me, taking a walk by the woods, a serene look on my face. The girl in the picture looked so happy—something I was not. I swallowed hard, trying to fight back the tears. I knew then that I would treasure that painting forever, and that even if I never saw it again, I would never be able to get it off my mind.

"It's beautiful," I managed to choke out. "Thank you, Yuri. I will treasure it forever, but I can't keep it. I'm sorry."

Should the Duke find it—and I had no delusions about being able to hide it from him—it would be my death. I shuddered at the thought of what he would put me through for simply possessing such an item.

Shaking, I quickly returned the gift to Yuri. No words could explain how much it was tearing me apart to do so. "Please understand... I cannot keep this. I simply can't."

I knew from the expression on his face that he was hurt that I wouldn't even take the gift from him, but what was I supposed to do? I couldn't bear the thought of having to go through what the Duke had put me through last time. My body might be able to handle it, but my mind would not.

Yuri took the piece of paper from me and nodded. "I understand."

Do you? Do you really understand?

I nodded toward him and began walking toward town. I expected him to leave me alone, but he didn't. He stayed quite a distance behind me, but he walked with me every step of the way.

Even I couldn't understand the profound effect that had on me. I was so grateful that he didn't leave me alone—that in his own way, he helped me defy the Duke. The Duke couldn't possibly punish me if Yuri chose to walk behind me the whole time.

I was wrong. The Duke punished me in the worst possible way.

The moment I got back to the manor, the Duke told me to get dressed. He was going to present me to someone else that night. I wondered then if he had finally tired of me and if I was going to be one of the common whores in his brothel. He instructed me to prepare myself to be as beautiful as I possibly could. That was never a good sign.

I didn't understand why he was doing this or what he had in store, but I knew without a doubt that I wasn't going to like it.

Just before I was brought to the Duke's client, the Duke put a mask on me.

"Keep it on until he's had his way with you, do you understand? I will know if you disobey me…"

I nodded. Though there was no way he could find out, I was too afraid of ever defying him.

Upon seeing the man I was going to pleasure that night, I realized immediately why the Duke saw the mask as necessary.

The client he gave me to was Yuri.

"You're thinking about that boy again," Ingrid said. She'd just returned from another one of her midnight rendezvouses.

I wondered how she did it… how she was able to shut off her love for Aiden. There were times when I'd had to push back any thoughts of Yuri—especially when I'd been with Ben—but I couldn't do it for long. I craved Yuri's company, his smile, his words and his presence.

Ingrid Maslen appealed to my desire for power and control, but something about her repelled me too. We were alike in so many ways—ruined by our past and feeling helpless to make good out of the ashes we'd risen up from. Staring at her that night, however, I realized that I didn't want to end up like her.

I have so much to make up for.

I was determined that things would be different. *I'm going to make it up to Yuri. I have to.*

A knock on the door interrupted my thoughts. It was the young hunter, Zinnia.

"Aiden's little princess wishes to see you," she said with disdain.

I was brought to the suite they kept Sofia in.

"Claudia," she greeted me with a tentative smile. "Please have a seat."

I could tell that she still wasn't certain if I was friend or foe. I took my seat and waited for her to speak up. I felt vulnerable and unsure of myself.

"I'm going to escape soon. I was allowed to see Ingrid and spend some time with her and, well, she showed me a way out."

My heart leapt, but from the expression on her face, I could tell that she had no intention of bringing me with her.

"It's too much of a risk to bring you with me, Claudia. They keep me locked up at night... The only way I can sneak out is in broad daylight... I just... I don't know how it would be possible to take you with me."

"Sofia, if they leave me here, they're going to kill me. You're the only reason I'm still alive."

"No." She shook her head. "Ben is the reason they're keeping you alive."

"I need to get back to The Shade, Sofia... You of all people should understand why."

"I understand that, Claudia, and I promise that I will do everything in my power to get you back home. I can talk Derek into finding a way to get you back."

I tried to smile. I knew Sofia was sincere in her promise, but no vampire who entered hunter territory ever got out, with the exception of Derek.

"I hope you succeed in your escape, Sofia. Don't forget about me when you do."

I actually meant it.

CHAPTER 18: SOFIA

Ingrid betrayed me.

I found the garden through the secret passageways Ingrid had told me about. I thought that I was free when I reached open air, only to find Aiden waiting for me.

"Ingrid told me you'd try to escape," he said through gritted teeth.

I wanted to tell him that it was Ingrid who had showed me the way, but I had the inkling that he might've already known that. *Why would she give me the means to escape only to rat me out to Aiden on the night of my escape?*

Aiden grabbed me by the arm and practically dragged me to my room. I sat back on the couch inside my living room, watching as Aiden paced the floor in front of me.

"I trusted you, Sofia," he said.

"Since when?" I practically spat the words. "You're keeping me prisoner here, Aiden. I want to go back to Derek."

"Forget him, Sofia. As long as I am alive, you and he will never be together!"

Tears brimmed as I shook my head. "You don't understand how impossible it is for me to forget Derek. We belong together. You don't know what's at stake as long as you keep us apart."

"If he wanted to be with you, Sofia, why isn't he here? Why did he leave? If he thought that it was better for you to be together than apart, why is he not making a move to get back to you?"

He was preying on my deepest fears, but I couldn't let him. I knew what I had with Derek was real. If Derek wasn't coming to me, then there was a damned good reason why and I wasn't about to sit there and doubt everything we had.

"Well?" Aiden pried, perhaps thinking that he had gained some ground with me.

"I believe in Derek in a way I could never bring myself to believe in you."

"What did that man feed you to make you so obsessed with him? Is it the fact that you've already gulped gallons of his blood or is it because you've willingly fed him gallons of yours? He is *immortal*, Sofia. How could you ever be together? Unless..." Aiden's eyes widened. "You've thought about it, haven't you? You've considered getting turned."

I ground my teeth. Exhausted by everything that was happening and consumed by my desire to be with Derek, I spat the truth out before I could bite my tongue. "Yes. I have. Not only have I considered it, I *have been* turned. Multiple times. Derek tried to turn me when he was still here with me, and yet here I am... still human."

Aiden's eyes widened with horror as he tried to process what I had just told him.

"Don't look so surprised, Father. It's not like you didn't know." I couldn't hide the spite in my voice. "You knew that the reason I was so sick after Camilla left was because she gave me to Borys Maslen as a child. He tried to turn me when I was nine years old so that I could be his forever, but he failed. Claudia tried to turn me back at The Oasis, but she failed. Derek tried to turn me. He, too, failed. So don't worry, Father. You never have to worry about me becoming one of the creatures you're trying to rid the planet of."

Aiden looked horrified. It became clear to me that he knew nothing about what I was talking about—about me being immune.

I creased my brows as we both stood at a standstill that seemed to last for eternity. "You didn't know," I eventually said.

"It's impossible." He shook his head. "How could that be true? How could anyone be immune from the curse?"

He was looking at me like I was some sort of rare specimen. I began to wonder what implications came with the news that I had just revealed.

"Sofia... You're immune from being a vampire? How is that possible?"

"Perhaps there's a cure..." I found myself voicing the thought that'd been circling my mind ever since Derek had failed to turn me. *Did he leave because he realized that I could never be immortal? Did he give up on us?* "What if there's a cure? I escaped vampirism... Maybe Derek can too."

Aiden shook his head. "No. There's no cure. Curses don't have cures." His voice choked and I could swear that a part of him wished that there indeed was a cure. "Stop this, Sofia. Stop buying into all these delusions that you can be with that bastard."

This time, it was my turn to be stubborn. "No, Aiden. I think there's a cure and trust me when I say I'm never going to stop until I find it. If it's the only way we can be together, then so be it. Derek will become immune too."

Chapter 19: Derek

I stared at Corrine, my mind reeling. *Don't you think I want that? Don't you think I want Sofia here with me?* But there was no way I could bring Sofia back. I didn't even know where hunter headquarters was.

"I want her here. You know that. But right now, I need to get The Shade back into shape... starting with this lockdown. I need the humans back at their posts before the island crumbles."

"And what if Felix and his men begin attacking people again?"

"I'll post guards at the Vale and all the other establishments to make sure nobody hurts the humans."

Corrine scoffed at this. "You're going to post vampires to stand guard over humans? Do you really think they'll agree to that?"

"They won't have a choice. I'm their king."

"They have a choice to join your father and Felix in rebellion. Besides, if you have the guards and knights posted mainly at the

Vale, how are you going to guard the Crimson Fortress, which we cannot, under any circumstances, allow your father's men to occupy?"

I was starting to get frustrated. Rosa was beginning to flinch. I decided to spare her from further discomfort. "Rosa, could you please get Sam, Kyle and Ashley here? Ian and Gavin too."

Her face lit up the moment I mentioned Gavin's name. I raised a brow in curiosity, and she most likely mistook it as me waiting for her to get out, so she practically leaped from her seat and mumbled something before going off.

"What do you want to happen, Corrine? Even if I could get Sofia back here, how is she going to help fix all this?"

Corrine gave me a look. Nobody at The Shade could make me feel as stupid as the brown-haired, olive-skinned witch could. "You're being a fool, Derek. Are you really that blind to the power Sofia has over the people of The Shade—especially the human population?"

I was taken aback. Humbling as it was, I had to admit that Corrine had a point. Sofia had a way about her that won trust and affection. The people of The Catacombs—Naturals or otherwise—listened to her.

"If she was here, then all you'd have to do is keep the vampires in check and she can do whatever magic she does with the humans. That's half of your work done for you."

"Even if that were true, I still haven't got the slightest clue how to bring Sofia here."

Right then, Ashley and Sam walked into the room, hands clasped. Kyle and Ian followed right after—glaring daggers at each other. Gavin followed after, seemingly deep in thought, while

Rosa trailed behind him.

"Finally," Ashley exclaimed as she and Sam plopped on the couch beside Corrine. "We're addressing the elephant in the room—how to get Sofia back here. Because let's face it, it's been a disaster without the two of you here calling the shots."

I narrowed my eyes at her. It came as a surprise to me that people around The Shade saw Sofia and me not as separate entities, but as a unit working together to rule The Shade.

"Well, I've been bugging him about it, but he seems to think it's hopeless," Corrine said.

Ashley stared at me thoughtfully. "Well, it kind of is…"

I was getting exhausted with the conversation. I wanted Sofia back. How could I not? But to go on and on about it, knowing that it was next to impossible for me to find her, was beginning to get irritating.

Ashley addressed me. "Do you remember where hawk headquarters is?"

I shook my head at the baby vampire. "No. You were once a hunter, Ashley. Don't you know where it is?"

"I never ranked high enough. I was blindfolded and escorted to headquarters whenever I needed to be there."

"They did the same thing to me. There's no way I can figure out where it is." We were at a dead end.

"Remind me again why you left her there." Ashley squinted at me.

I remembered when Ashley had still been human. I had allowed the darkness to consume me. I'd attacked her and fed on her several times. I'd craved her so much after I had first tasted her blood. *I left Sofia because I might do to her what I did to you.*

"I didn't call you here to discuss Sofia. We need to put a stop to this ridiculous lockdown. Gavin and Ian, you were working with Sofia as the human leaders of this place. What are your thoughts?"

Both men exchanged glances and Gavin was about to speak when Xavier showed up. "The lovely Natalie Borgia comes with a message." From behind him, Natalie emerged and stepped into the room.

I stood up and breathed a sigh of relief. "You're all right. I was certain that…"

Her eyes widened, warning me not to say anymore.

I restrained my urge to give her one big, grateful hug. "Your message?"

She eyed all the people present in the room. "This message contains sensitive information threatening the security of this island. You're sure you want everyone here to hear it?"

"They'll find out eventually," I assured her, steeling myself for the worst.

"The leaders of the other vampire covens want to meet with you."

It's a trap. Natalie wasn't her usual warm and inviting self. She was guarded. "If I don't go?"

"Why wouldn't you…" Xavier began to butt in.

I raised a hand to make him stop talking.

"If you don't go"—Natalie shifted her weight from one foot to the other—"they're going to attack The Shade."

"And if I go, they're going to capture me and most likely kill me, right?"

Her eyes softened, but she regained composure. "I guess you

have a decision to make, Derek."

I couldn't find a reason to go. I didn't have the slightest clue how the other vampires intended to orchestrate an attack on the island without being detected by the outside world.

"Tell them I need time to think about it. I'll let you know once I've made my decision."

Natalie handed me a sealed envelope. "The details of the meeting are in there." She gave me a long look.

"Thank you, Natalie." I tried to smile as I took the envelope. "For everything."

As if the world weren't already crashing in on me, Cameron showed up, a grave look on the Scot's freckled face.

"Cameron? What's wrong? Natalie was just about to leave the island."

"She can't," he said.

"What do you mean I can't?" Natalie frowned.

"Gregor and Felix just attacked the Port. They have control of it. I think they know that Natalie is here. They're making it look like you've taken her hostage."

I swallowed hard, knowing the implications of being accused of harming—in any way—a rogue vampire as important as Natalie. I eyed her, wondering if she had had any idea that this was coming. She seemed genuinely surprised.

"We need to take back control of the Port," Xavier mumbled.

The words had barely escaped his lips when a piercing scream echoed through the cavernous walls of The Catacombs.

Gavin, Ian and Kyle ran out of Sofia's quarters—located on the topmost level of the many layers of The Catacombs—and within minutes, only Gavin returned, announcing, "It's a riot. They're killing one another out there."

It was my first night back at The Shade.

Natalie stated the obvious. "Looks like your kingdom's falling apart, King Derek."

Chapter 20: Aiden

I held Ingrid's hand as we walked toward the garden where we had our now-regular midnight rendezvous—the same garden Sofia had discovered and tried to escape from. I was silent until we reached the garden, lost in thought, relieved that Ingrid wasn't trying to make conversation.

I knew the risk I was putting myself at by being in a relationship with her. The higher-ranking hunters had their eyes on me. The pressure I'd been getting for losing Derek Novak and for keeping vampires alive at headquarters was intense, but I couldn't do what they wanted me to do. I couldn't kill Claudia out of respect for Ben's last request. I couldn't kill Ingrid because the thought of my daughter suffering another death was beyond what I could handle.

Stop lying to yourself, Aiden. Ingrid is still alive because you can't stand the idea of losing your wife.

I let go of her hand, fully aware of how tightly I was clinging to our past. The nights I'd spent with Ingrid had been pure ecstasy—Ingrid was a passionate lover in a way that Camilla had never been.

That night, the moment we reached the garden, Ingrid motioned to kiss me, but I pushed her away. I stepped back, keeping a safe distance between her and me.

"How did Sofia know how to get to the garden?" I asked Ingrid.

Her shoulders sagged and she heaved a sigh. "She wanted to escape, Aiden. She asked me for help, so I helped her. My conscience couldn't stand it though. It felt like I was betraying you, so I had to tell you…"

I clenched my fists. "She's talking crazy. Sofia."

Delight sparked in Ingrid's eyes, but she covered that up. "Why do you say that?"

"She's talking about being immune to vampirism. She's talking about a cure to the curse." *I'm such a hypocrite. I'm condemning my daughter for loving a vampire, when I myself am in love with one.* I gave Ingrid a lingering look. *It's your curse too. How on earth could I allow myself to still love you?*

"Sofia and her delusions…" Ingrid sounded melancholy. "She thinks that because she's immune, there's some sort of cure that will make a lifetime of bliss possible for her and her beloved."

"Immune? She *is* immune?"

"Borys tried to turn her the night I gave her to him. She didn't turn. She's immune."

I couldn't wrap my mind around the idea that she could speak so nonchalantly about offering her nine-year-old daughter to a century-old vampire to turn. *How many times must I be reminded that she is not my Camilla?*

"Don't look at me like some monster, Aiden. It's not like you didn't know that I wanted Sofia to end up with Borys all those times we made love. Does it really make a difference now?" She drew close to me, pressing her body against mine.

This time, I pushed her away. "This ends now, Ingrid. No matter what we've been doing these past days, my loyalty remains with our daughter. You were right all along. You lost me to Sofia, and make no mistake about it, if she ever asks it of me, I wouldn't think twice about killing you."

Fury sparked in Ingrid's eyes as she bared her fangs.

I was a formidable hunter and compared to other vampires I'd fought before, a decade-old vampire was no match for me. As she was about to sink her teeth into my neck, I grabbed her head with both my hands and used all my strength to twist her head and snap her neck in two.

Quickest way to maim a vampire.

She dropped to the ground. She was still alive, but once I instructed someone to snap her neck back into place, she would realize that she had just lost all leverage she had gained from my renewal of love for her—or perhaps lust.

She was going to wake up in a dungeon, her fangs ripped from her mouth, regretting the day she had ever tried to harm my daughter.

CHAPTER 21: SOFIA

Aiden kept me locked in my bedroom. Zinnia came only to bring me food or take the dirty dishes away. She barely spoke to me or even looked at me.

"How long is he going to keep me here?" I asked after she had brought me breakfast on a tray. It was the morning of the second day after my botched escape attempt.

She glared at me. "Until you die, I hope. Ben gave up his life to get you safely back here, and this is how you repay him? By bolting back to that vampire boyfriend of yours the first chance you get?"

"You don't know Ben as well as I did, Zinnia. You weren't there with him at The Oasis. He didn't risk his life to get me back here. He gave it up so I could be happy, so I could be with Derek." I was choking up with tears at the memory of my best friend.

"Ben was loyal to the hunters. He never would've wanted you to end up with Derek."

"Really? Is that why he chose to stay with me at The Shade instead of returning here? Is that why he agreed to give me away on my wedding day, with Derek as my groom?"

Her eyes widened. "You married Derek Novak? Your father knows this?"

I shook my head. "I am engaged to Derek. I was abducted and taken to The Oasis before we could get married."

"What is wrong with you?"

"I don't need to explain myself to you. I want to see my father."

"He doesn't need to explain himself to you either. You may be Reuben's daughter, but you're nothing like him."

Thank heavens for that. I grimaced. I never could get used to what they called my father at hunter headquarters. *Reuben.* I wondered what kind of a life my father had lived even before my mother had become a vampire. *Aiden and Reuben—two sides of a coin, my father's double life—both sides a complete mystery to me.*

Zinnia left me with one final glare.

I didn't expect Aiden to arrive, knowing that Zinnia most likely wouldn't deliver my message to him, but later that afternoon, he stepped into the bedroom, looking rather uncomfortable.

"So Zinnia did send you my message."

"Zinnia didn't tell me anything… I just arrived from a business trip abroad. Has she been taking care of you?"

I was taken aback that he'd come to me of his own volition. "She's been feeding me regularly, if that's what you mean. I told her to let you know that I wanted to have a word with you."

"Well, what do you want to talk about?"

"You have to realize that I will jump at any chance I get to find Derek. You locking me up here only makes me want to do it more. That's like Raising Teenagers 101."

"You're eighteen, Sofia. Technically, you're already an adult."

"So treat me like one. Let me make my own decisions and my own mistakes. This is *my* life, a life you chose not to be a part of for the past nine years. Now that I make my own decisions, you can't just step in and call the shots."

One corner of his lips twitched. "I understand what you're saying, Sofia, but I'm doing what is best for you, and in that, I cannot waver. I know the vampires far better than you do, and in good conscience as your father, I cannot allow you to throw your life away because of this infatuation you have toward this creature. It doesn't matter how much you love him, Sofia. Your love doesn't keep him from being a monster."

There was so much sadness in his voice. I wondered once again if this reaction of his had anything to do with Ingrid knowing how to get to that garden. I crawled to the edge of the bed and sat on it. "Every day you keep me apart from him, you're killing a part of me."

He eyed me. "I can't give you what you want, but I can give you something close."

He pushed the door open and I couldn't help but gasp in horror when a young woman lurched into my room.

I blinked several times to make sure that I wasn't just seeing things, but sure enough, she was standing right there in front of me, a ghost from the past, someone I held close to my heart.

The Seer of The Shade herself.

Vivienne Novak.

Chapter 22: Derek

A lockdown that had morphed into a riot. A siege at the Port. A kingdom on the brink of civil war while facing an ongoing threat of an attack from outside forces.

Fabulous. Just fabulous.

After Natalie summed up the state of The Shade, I had no idea what to do other than to walk away.

"Where are you going?"

I didn't even know who among the people behind me asked the question. I didn't care anymore. I wasn't going to be able to quell the riot or retake the Port without bloodshed. The darkness was close to ruining me.

"I am going to take a drive."

"There's a riot and a siege going on, Derek." Xavier stepped forward. "Is this really the time to improve your driving skills?"

I pointed at Sam and Kyle. "You two work with Gavin and Ian

to figure out how to quell this stupid riot." I then pointed at Xavier and Cameron. "Call in all the vampires who are still with us. Those who want to remain neutral have that option. At least we'll know who is really with us. Come up with a plan of action on what to do about the siege at the Port." I cast a pleading look at the witch herself. "Corrine, please escort Natalie to The Sanctuary and treat her as our esteemed guest while she is stuck here at The Shade."

"What about me?" Ashley pointed at herself.

Of all the people present, she reminded me of Sofia the most and I knew that she would never shy away from speaking her mind. "Would you like to go on a joyride with me?"

A smile lit up the blonde's beautiful face. "Yes! Let's escape all this craziness." She looked Sam's way as if to ask his permission. He let her go, more perhaps out of respect for me than trust for either one of us.

"Derek, we need you to be a leader right now," Cameron said desperately. "This is no time for…"

"Let him go," Corrine cut him off. "He needs to win the battle inside before he can win the war with the outward forces."

I gave her a grateful look. She understood what the separation from Sofia was doing to me.

Of course, none of them dared to question the witch. The entire island's security was on her shoulders. Corrine rarely imposed her opinions on us, but when she did, we dared not cross her.

Ashley and I made our way to a wide open field west of the island where a red convertible was located. We used it for practice drives or whenever we just wanted to feel the night air blowing against our faces. It usually was Sofia seated on the passenger's seat beside me, screeching her lungs out, often reminding me that she wasn't immortal and that she was likely going to get killed. I didn't care much about the driving as much as I enjoyed her reaction.

"You miss her, don't you?" Ashley asked me after we settled into our seats.

I gripped the steering wheel hard.

"I've had her blood, Ashley."

Ashley gasped.

"She made me drink it to heal me quicker after Borys tortured me. I didn't want to, but... I crave her so much. I could barely think straight."

"I know Sofia. She would let you have all the blood you want. That's how much she loves you."

"I know. That's exactly what she did when she offered her neck up to me back at hawk territory. I knew then that this couldn't possibly work. Corrine keeps telling me to get Sofia back, but how? What kind of man would I be to prey on her? She doesn't deserve that."

"You see... that's just it. There was a time when you wouldn't have given a damn if it was wrong or right. You didn't have any qualms about sucking blood out of a woman. Why then are you so resistant to having Sofia's blood when she so willingly offers it to you?"

"Were you not listening to me?" I slammed my palms over the steering wheel in frustration. "I love her! I can't keep doing that to her!"

Ashley twisted her slim body on the passenger seat so she

could face me. "If there's anyone who's stood witness to the love you two have for each other, it's me. Sofia took a wooden stake for you, Derek—one that I tried to stab you with. You went against your own father and took countless lashes on her behalf. It's hard to believe that this is what's going to tear the two of you apart. It's madness. Bring this place back to some semblance of sanity, get back control of the Port and find a way to get Sofia back here. I'm sure if we put our heads together, we could narrow down the search and find the hunter territory."

"She's not coming back. We should just accept that." Even as I said the words, I found it hard to swallow. "Besides, what kind of a life would she live if she returned? What if I end up destroying her?"

"What if the love you have for each other is powerful enough to keep that from happening?" Ashley shot back. "Don't be a fool, Derek. Whether you admit it or not, you can't survive without her, so you might as well stop acting like a sap and get her back."

I didn't have a response. I knew what Ashley was saying was true.

"Let's go back."

"We're no longer going for a drive?" Ashley asked, tapping her palms over the dashboard.

"No." I shook my head. "We have a riot to stop and a Port to retake. Get ready for a fight, baby vamp."

Her face lit up in a wide grin. "That's what I'm talking about!"

At that moment, I remembered a promise I'd given Sofia not too long ago, a promise that came with the heart-shaped diamond pendant I had given to her as a gift. *Take it as a promise from me— a promise that I will find a way to be with you.*

I wondered if this would be a promise I had to break.

Chapter 23: Sofia

"Sofia..." Tears began rushing down Vivienne's face. She stumbled forward as I stood up from the bed to embrace her.

When we hugged, I realized how thin she was, how emaciated. Her skin was deathly pale and lacking all luster. Her lips were chapped and dry and she had scars all over her arms.

"What have they done to you?" I whispered.

She shook her head. "Nothing. They've been good to me, Sofia. I'm really glad to see you again. Have they been treating you well?"

We pulled apart from each other and I gave my father a suspicious look. "Yes, I'm fine. We thought you were dead, Vivienne. We had a ceremony for you at the Vale and everything."

She stared blankly at me. "Dead? Me? Of course not... I just... Well, it doesn't matter. You're here now." She grabbed my hand and pulled me toward a set of two couches with a round coffee table near the windows. "Let's catch up. Tell me everything that's been going on since you came here to headquarters."

I sat uncomfortably, wondering what was wrong with Vivienne.

My father nodded my way. "I'll leave you two to catch up."

I couldn't help but frown as he left without waiting for my consent. Back at The Shade, Vivienne had been serene. This Vivienne was antsy and anxious. My stomach knotted. *What have they done to you, Vivienne?*

"Derek was a mess after he found out that you died. He almost killed Ashley because the darkness took over him. What's happened to you?"

"Derek..." She shook her head slowly. "I was wrong about him, Sofia. I thought he was some sort of savior. I never should've helped you return to The Shade." She gripped my hands. "I'm so sorry, Sofia. I'm sorry for anything he might've put you through after you returned."

"Vivienne, Derek has been good to me. He loves me. You know that."

"I understand. It's going to take a while before you can recover from the trauma he's put you through. The denial is natural."

I was trying my hardest not to slap her across the face. *What has gotten into you?* "We're talking about Derek, Vivienne. Your twin. The same man who rescued you from Borys Maslen."

Horror showed in her eyes. "They told me that Borys got to you too. That's why we need to stay here, Sofia. If Borys gets his hands on you, it's going to be so much worse than what you had to go through with Derek."

"What have they done to you? It's like you've been brainwashed..."

Her brilliant blue eyes settled on me with so much compassion. "No, Sofia, it's you who's been brainwashed."

I couldn't help but laugh. "Is that what my father thinks, Vivienne? That I was brainwashed at The Shade so I would love Derek?" *This isn't her. This is just a shell spouting out words placed there by other people.* "You look tired, Vivienne."

She heaved a sigh and nodded. "That's because I am."

"Would you like to lie down and rest?" I waved an arm toward the bed.

She looked at the bed longingly. "Yes, please, and if I could have more blood… I'm thirsty."

"I'll make sure they bring you some. Is there anything else you need?"

She shook her head as she stood up and dragged herself to the bed. Without another word, she laid her head on the pillow. Within a couple of minutes, she was fast asleep.

She slept for hours.

Zinnia entered to bring me breakfast just as I pulled the drapes over the windows to protect Vivienne from the sunlight.

Zinnia stared with disdain at Vivienne.

"What have you guys been doing to her? She's not the Vivienne I knew back at The Shade…"

Zinnia shrugged. "I thought she was dead. Even Ben thought she was dead. He was the last one to interrogate and torture her before what was supposed to be her execution."

I gulped at the idea of Ben torturing Vivienne. As much as I wanted not to believe it, I knew how much he'd hated vampires after what Claudia had put him through at The Shade. It was the reason he'd become a hunter in the first place.

"So you admit it… She was tortured."

Zinnia smirked. "What do you think vampires go through here, Sofia? They are interrogated and tortured for any information about their covens, and once we get as much as we can from them, we have them executed—the exact same thing your mother is going through right now."

My face paled. "Ingrid?"

"After the stunt she pulled helping you escape, she fell from Reuben's good graces."

"May I see her?"

Zinnia shrugged. "Reuben's calling all the shots, but if he goes on keeping all these vamps alive, I doubt the authorities will tolerate it much longer."

It had never dawned on me that he could get in trouble for what he was doing.

"Zinnia," I called out just as she was about to leave. "Could you have some blood brought in for Vivienne, please?"

"Why?" she asked.

"Because if you don't, I might have to feed her mine. Look at her… She looks awful."

"What is with you and treating your blood like it's orange juice?" Zinnia shook her head in exasperation. "She can't suck your blood. Her fangs have been pulled out."

"Well, can't I just cut myself and make her drink the blood I drain out of myself?"

"You're insane. It baffles me still how you could be in any way related to Reuben. All we have is animal blood."

"That's fine. Vivienne is used to animal blood."

Zinnia rolled her eyes and turned her back on me. I was sure that she wasn't going to fulfill my request, but when she returned for my breakfast dishes, she had two glasses of blood with her.

It took another couple of hours before Vivienne began stirring. At first, I ignored her, thinking that she was just having a dream. All of a sudden she began to take erratic, heavy breaths. She started whimpering and it didn't take long before the whimpers turned into screams, tears running down her cheeks.

I rushed to her side and began shaking her awake. "Vivienne! Wake up!"

She jolted up in bed. She set her eyes on me and sighed with relief before she broke out into sobs. "Sofia... you're here."

"Yes... I'm here." I pulled her into a tight embrace.

Trembling, she whispered into my ear. "You still have my memories, don't you, Sofia? Please... please..."

She paused and I found myself holding my breath as I awaited her request. "What is it, Vivienne? What do you want from me?"

"Remind me who I am."

CHAPTER 24: AIDEN

From the control center's surveillance monitor, I watched the two women share an embrace. *This isn't working out. Vivienne is supposed to sway Sofia to our side. Instead, it seems Sofia is about to restore her to her old, stubborn self.*

Zinnia stepped beside me as we watched the scene in my daughter's bedroom.

"What was that about?" I reprimanded her.

"What?" she asked, feigning innocence.

"Why that talk to Sofia about what was done to Ingrid? Don't ever mention Ingrid to her again, Zinnia. I can see that you're not a big fan of my daughter, but she's *my* daughter. It will do you well not to mess with her."

Zinnia rolled her eyes. "I didn't sign up to become a hunter just so I could babysit your daughter and bring her meals."

"Patience, Zinnia. When this is all over, your next mission will be Derek Novak and The Shade."

"How? Vivienne isn't acting the way she's supposed to. It's like there's something about your daughter."

"No one has ever broken through our brainwashing."

"Well, Sofia seems to be doing a great job at it. Vivienne started acting erratically the moment she was presented to Sofia."

"I think I'm going about this the wrong way." I hated to admit it, but there was no sign that Sofia had ever been brainwashed by the Novaks. I was just telling myself that because I couldn't bring myself to accept the fact that her loyalty toward Derek and The Shade was genuine.

Perhaps she really does love him.

Derek and Sofia are genuinely in love.

I focused on the image on the screen, trying to make sense of the words Sofia was uttering to remind Vivienne of the past, a past I was surprised Sofia was so well acquainted with.

There was talk of a shipwreck and first blood, of massacres and cullings and centuries of trying to preserve their own kind against us. Coming from my daughter's own lips, it was almost like we were the villains and the vampires were the victims.

Vivienne was a blank slate until my daughter mentioned a greenhouse. At this, Vivienne's eyes lit up. "Is it still beautiful?" she asked in a whisper, as if saying it too loud would somehow destroy the beauty of it.

Sofia broke into a smile. "Yes, Viv. It's still gorgeous. Derek took care of it after you disappeared. He made sure it would be as beautiful as it would be if you were there."

Vivienne's next words sealed reality for me. I'd just lost Vivienne to Sofia.

"I miss Derek so much," Vivienne confessed, a tear running down her cheek.

"Well, that was a huge waste of time." Zinnia smirked.

I clenched my fists.

"What are you going to do now, Reuben?"

"I think I need to take a different approach. I have to accept that Sofia really does love Derek Novak and there's no way I can sway her from that."

"So you're just going to keep her locked in that room until she gets over him?"

"No. She'll hate me forever if I do that. The best thing for me to do right now is to give her exactly what she wants."

"You're giving her to Derek Novak?"

I shook my head. A plan began to take form in my mind. "No. I'm going to give her a cure to vampirism."

Chapter 25: Derek

When Ashley and I arrived at The Catacombs, it was in total chaos. I'd just walked into one of the levels that lined the circular pit in the middle of the caves when a bottle was thrown my way. I dodged it, but blood trickled from Ashley's forehead.

"Ow." She brushed off any remaining pieces of broken glass from her forehead.

I couldn't help but let out a wry laugh. "Welcome to The Catacombs, Ash."

She rolled her eyes. "Wipe that smirk off your face, Novak." She picked up a shard of glass from the broken bottle and pointed it at me. "I don't care that you're most likely a hundred times stronger than me, I can still cut you."

I grinned. "Scary. Let's end this riot before some other flying object breaks your neck." I leaned over the wooden banister that overlooked the rest of The Catacombs' levels. I still had no idea what they were even fighting over.

Kyle, holding a frightened Anna by the arm, dragged her to what I assumed was Sofia's quarters. Ian was about a hundred meters behind them, trying to keep up.

Gavin hit another guy who had just lunged at him. Rosa, on the other hand, daintily hit a man in the back of his neck with a glass bottle. The man had been about to attack Gavin, who seemed intent on finding his family.

I practically jumped out of my skin when I felt a tap on my back. My immediate reflex was to grab whoever had just touched me by the neck.

Sam raised both hands. "Relax. It's me."

"What's going on?" I demanded as I pulled my hand away from his neck. "You were supposed to quell the riot."

He pulled Ashley into his arms before shrugging. "It's not like we have any authority here at The Catacombs or in The Shade. These people aren't listening to us."

"Do you even know why they're rioting or what they're demanding?"

Sam was about to open his mouth to answer me, but someone screamed "Fire!"

Sure enough, on the level below ours, where Gavin and Rosa were, a fire had just erupted. Gavin's eyes grew wide with panic. "Mother!" he screamed. He frantically searched his surroundings in search of Lily and the children.

That was when he caught sight of me. His jaw tightened as he gave me a pleading look.

It took all the strength I had to conjure up a voice loud enough to drown out the chaos going on around me.

"ENOUGH!"

The word echoed throughout the entire place and an immediate hush followed. All eyes turned toward me.

"Get water and stop that fire." I pointed toward the flames. "If you don't do as I say, we won't need a culling to end all your lives. You will die of suffocation if you don't murder yourselves first."

Immediately, everyone's focus shifted from their fist fights and ridiculous differences to the fire that was now threatening to kill them all. Gavin shot me a thankful look as he once again went about finding his family, Rosa helping him like a wide-eyed puppy.

"Rosa has a thing for Gavin, doesn't she?" I asked.

Ashley and Sam chuckled.

"The only person who can't seem to figure it out is Gavin, who is probably one of the densest people I've ever come across," Ashley said.

We watched as everyone worked hand in hand, passing buckets of water and sackcloth to try to save their homes. No questions asked. The fire would soon die with few or no casualties.

All that was required was to get them to listen to one voice. I realized then what was the matter. The Naturals were used to being slaves. They were used to being told what to do. Left to themselves, what resulted was anarchy.

Corrine could've quelled this riot easily, but she never meddled with things that she wasn't personally invested in. In her eyes, this was my problem and I needed to find a solution to it.

Truth be told, I wanted to just threaten to kill them all, but Sofia would try to find the solution that would lead to the most lives spared.

I waited until the fire had been completely put out before speaking up. "Who is going to answer to me for this riot? What is going on? This is madness!"

I was met with utter silence.

"This riot and the lockdown are over. If you want to discuss what you want, there will be a meeting tomorrow at the Vale's town square. If you don't show up, you forfeit your right to be heard."

"You just want us out so it will be easier to kill us all!" some anonymous voice hidden among the crowd cried out.

"If I wanted you dead, you'd be dead," I bellowed. "Besides, you're doing a pretty good job at killing yourselves all on your own. The day after tomorrow, I expect everyone to be back at their posts, doing their work. If you have issues with this, then take it up directly with me."

I began to walk toward the exit of The Catacombs.

"I guess that ends that," Sam muttered under his breath as he and Ashley followed behind me.

I heaved a sigh.

"No, Sam. This is barely the beginning."

CHAPTER 26: SOFIA

I gently shut the door to my bedroom as I stepped out into the living room, relieved that I was no longer being kept prisoner in one room.

My father sat on one of the wooden bar stools taking a swig of Scotch. I stared at him for a couple of seconds before moving forward. I didn't know what to say to him, so I was relieved when he broke the silence.

"How's Vivienne?"

"She was finally able to get back to sleep. She's better now." *No thanks to you.* I climbed onto one of the stools next to him. "Why are you here, Aiden?"

"I came to discuss something of importance with you…"

My thoughts began to drift to all the vampires who'd been tortured and killed at headquarters. I couldn't point out the difference between Aiden and the vampires back at The Shade who treated their captives as prey.

"Sofia, are you even listening to me?" He snapped his fingers in front of my face.

"Is it true that you're now doing to Ingrid what you did to Vivienne? You pulled out Vivienne's fangs. Do you do that to all vampires? Is that what you're going to do to Claudia too? I've seen her hurt many humans, but torturing her in that manner seems… inhumane."

"Inhumane? Are you listening to yourself, Sofia? These creatures aren't humans. Nothing you do to them can be inhumane."

I couldn't believe my ears. *Does he truly believe that?* "I want to see Ingrid. I don't care if she's a crazy freak trying to pawn me off on a vampire even crazier than her. She's still my mother and the idea of you doing to her what you did to Vivienne…" I choked on my words. *How could anyone with a conscience treat others this way?*

"You're willing to just forget everything Ingrid did to you? To us?"

"I couldn't forget even if I wanted to, Aiden. You both scarred me for life when you both abandoned me. She's done worse things, but you are still guilty. Where were you that night when she came with Borys? Why was I home alone? I've been wronged by both of you, by so many other people—vampires and humans alike. That doesn't mean I want to go around torturing and killing everyone who's wronged me!"

Aiden looked taken aback by my outburst. He opened his mouth, but shut it again.

I was fighting the urge to cry. I was tired of being the victim. Whether I was at The Shade or back in California with the

Hudsons or here with the hunters, I was always the one in need of saving. *I'm sick of it. This time, it's my turn to rescue someone.* The thought came with so much conviction, I actually slammed my palm on the counter, making my father jolt back in surprise.

"Sofia, I..." His voice came with a squeak. Tears were beginning to brim in his eyes.

I stared at him, horrified. All those years growing up, I had wished that he would just look my way, let me know that I was precious to him, but he'd never been there. I had rehearsed so many times what I would say to him if I got the chance to confront him and let him know how much he'd broken me by leaving me. Now that I'd already done that, I couldn't stand it. I couldn't stand hurting my father.

This is exactly why I can't understand the path of vengeance. No matter how much someone has hurt me, I still find no pleasure in seeing them hurt.

He managed to compose himself. "I never said sorry for leaving you. I thought it was the best thing to do. I know that's no excuse for not being the father you needed, but I couldn't look at you without thinking of your mother. I couldn't even be in the same room with you. After I left you with the Hudsons, I... I just... I got in deep with the hunters. I didn't want you to be a part of that world. I thought that I was keeping you safe by leaving you with them. I thought that maybe, just maybe... you could have some semblance of a normal life." He gripped my hand and squeezed tightly. "I'm sorry, Sofia. Believe me. I truly want to make it up to you."

Overcome by emotion, I got off my seat and hugged him. "You have no idea how much your apology means to me," I whispered into his ear before placing a kiss on his cheek.

He wrapped his arms around me and hugged me back. "You're my little girl, Sofia. My precious daughter. I may have a crappy way of showing it, but I love you."

He kissed my forehead and it was all I could do to keep myself from breaking down into sobs. I relished that embrace for a couple more minutes before finally pulling away from him.

We'd made a connection only a father and daughter could have. However, we were still keenly aware of our differences.

With him already having heard my rants, I figured it was time I listened to what he was trying to tell me. "So what were you saying before I interrupted?"

"I was trying to tell you that you may be right. There just might be a cure to vampirism."

My breath hitched. I couldn't believe my ears. *Why wasn't I listening the first time?* Suddenly, I found myself holding my breath, hanging on to his every word.

"If you're immune, then maybe there's something in your DNA that makes you immune to the curse. If it's all right with you, I'm going to have some of our scientists get a sample of your blood and we'll see where that takes us."

I stared at him, hope unlike any I'd known before rising up within me. *This is it. This is the way Derek and I can be together.*

"Sofia? What do you say?"

I nodded emphatically. "Yes. Yes. I'll give you whatever you need." Before I could hold myself back, I threw my arms around his neck a second time. For the first time in eighteen years, it felt like I had a father who cared. I'd never been more thankful that Aiden Claremont was my dad.

"Thank you! Thank you so much!"

"I love you, Sofia. Don't you ever forget that."

"I love you too... Dad."

CHAPTER 27: DEREK

"We're in the middle of a siege at the Port and you pick tomorrow to call a general assembly at the town square?"

Xavier was never one to treat me like the king The Shade portrayed me to be, but in this case, he really wasn't throwing any deference my way. In fact, as he paced the floor of the room at the Crimson Fortress, he was talking to me like a father scolding his teenage son.

I took my seat at the head of the table where Cameron and Liana, Eli and Yuri were already seated. Xavier, of course, was still on his feet, but his words barely registered in my mind. It was mostly about me losing my mind and that he'd known from the beginning that I was crazy.

"And yet here you are, still fighting by my side."

That halted him and the man paused to give me a pensive look. "Yes... well, you may be crazy, but the times you are brilliant make up for it."

"Finally." I threw my hands in the air. "A compliment. Now, could you kindly take a seat so we can get to business?"

Xander begrudgingly sat down before drumming his fingers on the table.

"We have three orders of business," I began. "One, the general assembly. Two, the siege at the Port. Three, the fact that it looks like we're holding Natalie hostage."

"Can't Natalie send a message to the covens that there's a siege going on?" Liana suggested. "I'm sure she knows of a way to contact the other covens from within the island."

I shook my head. "I'm sure she does, but the other covens are threatening to attack us. Is it really the best course to let them know that we're on the brink of civil war? It's exposing too much of our weaknesses."

"We have to retake the Port as soon as possible then." Cameron concluded with the obvious.

"Right." I nodded. "How?"

"Let's just go in guns blazing—so to speak—and kill everyone. The island would be better off without the likes of them if you ask me," Xavier said, always the hothead.

Perhaps that's why Xavier and I get along so well. We're both so trigger-happy. "We can't afford to do that. We have to do this with as little bloodshed as possible." In this, I was firm.

"Why?" Yuri spat. "They've betrayed you. They're out to ruin The Shade."

I straightened up on my seat. "These men fought and bled with us through First Blood. They may be misguided by whatever lies my father weaved to discredit me, but if we are to reach true sanctuary then we have to find a way to work together. Our military force is paralyzed without them. If the other covens attack without them on our side, it will be the end of us."

Silence ensued.

Xavier broke the silence. "Why is the general assembly necessary? And at the town square, Derek? The humans would be like sitting ducks there. What if Gregor and Felix attack?"

"What would they do?" Liana interjected. "Murder the entire human population? Even Felix isn't stupid enough to do that. Let's not forget that he once advocated better rights for the humans..."

"That's because he was still in love with Anna at that time." Yuri waved her comment off. "I honestly think that he wouldn't mind killing her now."

"Wait." Eli lifted his glasses over the bridge of his nose. I could practically see the wheels turning. "This could work to our advantage. If we could lure some of the vampires at the Port into the assembly, then we'd have a better chance of taking over the Port."

"We still won't be able to get in." Xavier shook his head. "They'll attack us the moment we're at the narrow staircase."

"No, no... This can work. We don't have to pass through there. The Port isn't the only way out of the island." I swallowed hard. The Lighthouse was my long-kept secret. Only Vivienne and Sofia were aware of it. The shore near the Lighthouse was where Cora and I had drifted to the island from the shipwreck we'd survived five hundred years ago. Aside from the Port and that small patch of shore near the Lighthouse, the island was surrounded by rocky boulders and cliffs.

All eyes were on me as they waited with bated breath.

"First off all," I began, "who knows how to swim?"

Gregor Novak won't know what hit him.

Chapter 28: Sofia

Aiden escorted me to where they were keeping Ingrid. Anxious wasn't a strong enough word to describe how I felt about seeing Ingrid again. I fumbled with my fingers, wondering why on earth she had such an effect on me.

She's your mother, Sofia. If what Zinnia was saying is true, then you're about to see a tortured version of her—the same way Vivienne looks now. The idea made me sick to my stomach. No matter what Ingrid did, no matter how insane she was, to me, she would always be Camilla Claremont.

I gave my father a glance, wondering if he felt the same way. A wave of nostalgia hit me as I remembered what coming home from school was like when we were still a family.

He always came on time. Whenever the school bell rang and I ran down the front steps of the red-brick school that I went to for my elementary education, I could always expect the black BMW waiting for me in the parking lot.

My dad would be leaning against the passenger side door, arms crossed over his chest and a big smile on his face.

"Hello, baby," he greeted me, before taking my backpack and putting it on the passenger's seat. "Would you like some ice cream?"

"Yes!"

He would tell me to hush and not tell my mother, but once we reached home, I would tell her anyway and he would make a mess out of my hair for getting him into trouble.

After the afternoon snack, we would drive home together and he would ask me how my day was. He never once made me feel like he wasn't listening. He always seemed genuinely interested.

More often than not, once we got home, we would find my mother in the kitchen or in her study. I loved her study. There were so many trinkets and artifacts in there. Every one had a fascinating story. The Red Orb was my favorite. My dad said that it was how he had gotten my mother to fall in love with him. I loved that story.

Dinner was never without laughter, and there were always plenty of hugs and kisses to go around. I was a happy child. I felt loved. I never would've imagined that things would turn out the way that they did.

I'd always felt like Aiden had adored me and I still couldn't wrap my mind around the idea that Camilla had held any form of resentment toward me. We'd been a picture-perfect family. Perhaps that was why it had been so traumatic for me when they had abandoned me. It didn't help that growing up, I'd been diagnosed with many psychological disorders—ranging from ADHD to OCD. It wasn't until I'd reached The Shade that Corrine had figured out I had LLI or Low Latent Inhibition. It heightened my senses. I could hear, see, feel, sense everything going on around me intensely. I wondered if this was the reason I felt deeply for those in pain.

I shuddered when I remembered Derek in the dungeons of The Oasis. I knew then that I would rather die than be held captive by Borys Maslen again.

"You're shaking, Sofia." Aiden broke through my thoughts. "Nervous?"

I nodded. "Kind of. I'm always antsy whenever I have to see Ingrid. She says the most disturbing things sometimes. Trips to her demented mind are never pleasant."

Aiden chuckled. "That's true," he said, the hint of bitterness in his voice hard to miss.

"Do you love her still?" I asked.

He gave me a look as if to wonder if he ought to answer my question. He bowed his head and nodded. "I think I always will."

I could sense his sadness. I would never understand how my mother could've let go of him and what we had together as a family.

By the time we reached Ingrid's cell, I really couldn't think about anything other than the question, *Why?*

When we showed up and the lights were turned on inside her cell, I was surprised by her appearance. She didn't look as awful as Vivienne, but based on the bloodstains lining her mouth, her fangs had already been ripped out. Scientists milled around her. They had her strapped to the cot so she wasn't able to move.

Ingrid raised her eyes, and a manic grin—that would most likely haunt my nightmares—formed on her face. "Well, look who came for a visit. Aiden and his beloved Sofia... To what do I owe the honor of your presence? Once again, it looks like I failed to tear you two apart."

I grimaced, not even certain if I wanted to know what was going through her demented mind. I stared at her, wondering if what we were about to do was right. *Of course it is. How could it not be?*

Aiden ignored Ingrid and turned to me. "They have been prepping her system, making sure all her vitals are as required. I'm going to administer the final stage of the process." He pulled out a syringe and began shaking it.

"How does this even work?" I asked, feeling a knot form in my stomach.

"We mixed the samples of blood that you gave us with vampire blood. Something in your blood began to battle something in the vampire's blood. Of course, nothing happened, or should we say nobody won, until we put the mixture through a heating process and added saricis root to the mixture…"

Ingrid had been listening and horror showed in her eyes when she realized what was about to occur. She once again fought against her restraints.

"You sure you want to see this?" Aiden asked me.

I nodded, although I wasn't feeling as confident as I might've put on. "I wouldn't miss it for the world."

Wide-eyed terror flashed into Ingrid's face. "What are you going to do to me?"

"Relax, honey." My father tried to soothe her.

The scientists surrounding her stepped aside as she writhed against her restraints on the bed. "What's that? What's it for?" She stared at the syringe like it was about to bite her.

That's exactly what it will do. Or perhaps it's more accurate to say that it will reverse the effects of a bite.

In my father's hands was the cure, and if the hunters' scientists had got it right, I was about to watch Ingrid Maslen turn back into Camilla Claremont—whether she wanted to or not.

Chapter 29: Gregor

The general assembly was far too tempting to pass up. I hadn't had fresh human blood in weeks and the idea that the lockdown was over and I could just grab any person at random and drain the blood out of them was hard not to bite into.

"It could be a trap," I told Felix.

We were at the Port's control center, trying to figure out how we were going to keep ourselves fed. The moment we'd realized that we'd begun the siege with just a few packets of blood to keep us from starvation, I knew that there was a possibility that Derek would just wait us out until we came out desperate for blood. Thus, I was pleased to find out that Natalie Borgia was on the island and keeping her hostage wouldn't bode well for Derek at all.

Felix shook his head. "One of my men was there when Derek stopped the riot. He swore that Derek just came up with it on the spur of the moment. Besides, what are they going to do?"

I stared at Felix, wondering if I could trust what he was saying. He wasn't the greatest strategic mind. *Here was I hoping Eli was on my side.* I grimaced, once again feeling the pain of betrayal upon realizing that my own subjects—ones I'd served for four hundred years while my son slept like a baby—could turn their backs on me. *What I would do to them should I ever regain my power... They're going to pay. I swear it.*

"I don't get it," one of Felix's men muttered. "Derek could easily just speed down here and kill us all. Why doesn't he just do that?"

I raised a brow at him. "Derek Novak isn't that powerful. I sired him. I am more powerful than he is."

Obviously, he had something to say to that too, but he shut his mouth. *Smart boy.*

"So what are we going to do?" Felix asked.

"We get ourselves a bunch of humans to prey on. Let's see Derek quell another riot after we do that."

Our plan seemed perfect. Divide up the men. Some would hold the Port, while the others would stake out the pathways that led from The Catacombs to the Vale. We didn't need to attack the town square. All we had to do was create panic by killing the humans while they were on their way to the assembly.

I wanted blood, so I chose to be with the group that would stake out the humans. Felix stayed behind to lead the guarding of the Port.

As I hid myself behind a tree trunk from which the opening to the Black Heights was visible, pleasure built up inside of me at the mere thought of once again drinking fresh human blood from a beating heart, pumping the liquid right into my parched throat.

I wasn't sure if I would be able to keep myself from jumping at the first human who emerged from the cave. We had to let a number of them come out and pass through before we could attack. We couldn't afford to have them warn those who followed after. I had to hold back my anticipation as we waited. Then waited some more.

It felt like an eternity. I hadn't laid eyes on a single human. Once I realized that none of the humans were about to emerge from the caves, I was livid. "Let's go in," I announced out of pure impulse.

"Are you sure?" one of the men I was with asked. "What if there are vampire guards in there? The humans could still be in a lockdown. It wouldn't be the first time Felix would be wrong."

A slew of curses escaped from my lips. "I don't care! I want blood and I am going to get it!"

I should've learned my lesson. Anything I did out of pure impulse usually got me into trouble. We stormed the opening of the Black Heights and, sure enough, the entrance that led to The Catacombs was sealed. *They're still in lockdown. How?*

I turned to the other side—to the area of the mountain caves that led to The Cells, the island's prison system. My heart sank when Xavier emerged with twice as many men as I had. Outside, Yuri led another group of vampires.

"Do you really want to die tonight?" Xavier cocked his head to the side. "Because I don't share Derek's belief that we ought to keep you alive. I really don't mind ending your lives."

"You insolent son of a…" I began to spit out, but paused mid-sentence when the men surrounding me began lifting their hands in surrender. "You cowards! The lot of you! All bloody cowards!"

I attacked Xavier and we crashed to the ground. I was about to rip his heart out, but I was immediately held back by the other men.

I knew I looked like a manic fool shouting curses, but I didn't care. I hated the idea that Derek had once again outsmarted me. The humiliation was more painful than the betrayal.

"It doesn't matter. We still hold the Port!"

At that, Yuri scoffed. "I wouldn't say that. Derek's a pretty good swimmer. So are Cameron and Liana." He narrowed his eyes. "Wasn't it Cameron who rescued you from that shipwreck five hundred years ago?"

"I'm going to kill you! I'm going to kill you all!"

For the first time since I had established The Shade, I spent the night as a prisoner of the kingdom that I ruled. Sitting in a dungeon at The Cell, I was on the brink of insanity.

How could my own son do this to me? Doesn't he realize that if I fail at my mission to take over The Shade, it will be the end of me?

I was whimpering like a child. How could I not? The darkness was never kind to those who failed.

This is it.

He may not know it yet, but Derek just murdered his own father.

Chapter 30: Derek

Felix's face was priceless. He clearly never saw it coming. The swim from the shore of the Lighthouse to the underwater portals of the Port had been long and exhausting, but all we had to do was stealthily get from the portals we used to get people transferred from the submarines to the Port and recover our strength inside one of the submarines.

Felix and his men were lax in their guarding of the Port, thinking the only way we could get in was through the staircase. Thus, when Cameron, Liana and I emerged from one of the submarines, they all looked shocked.

Felix, whom I'd always known was a coward, made a run for it. Those who weren't able to run surrendered. It seemed none of them were willing to die for whatever cause they were fighting for. I breathed out a sigh, hoping that Xavier and Yuri had been able to take my father by surprise too.

After we had finished our planning at the Crimson Fortress, we'd decided to postpone the general assembly. I'd instructed Gavin and Ian to spread the word that the general assembly was to be at a later date and that they were once again on lockdown until we could eliminate the threat Felix and Gregor posed to them.

What I would've given to see the reaction on my father's face upon realizing that The Catacombs was still on lockdown.

I had just walked out of the Port to breathe in the fresh night air when a familiar voice called my name.

"You did it." Corrine said as she approached with Natalie. As I turned to face the witch, I was surprised to see her smiling. Corrine always seemed to have a look of disapproval on her face.

"*We* did it," I clarified, although I wasn't exactly sure what it was that we'd done. We'd regained control of the Port and the riot at The Catacombs was over, but I still had to figure out how to get to Sofia and there was still a threat of attack from the other covens.

"I'll try to get a response back to the covens as soon as possible." Natalie gazed at me with concern, as if to ask me if I was sure I wanted to meet with the other coven leaders.

I couldn't help but wonder if there was some way she was being heard by the other covens. She seemed to be extremely guarded with what she said.

She embraced me and whispered, "Don't go," so softly, I barely heard it.

I nodded. "I've been thinking about the meeting and I think it would be better if my father goes on my behalf. He's usually the one who speaks to the other coven leaders. He once was the ruler of The Shade. He's more capable of handling these things than me." *And if Gregor goes, that means I won't have to worry about him messing things up here at The Shade.*

"Derek, they want you." Natalie shook her head. "If you don't go, then they are going to attack."

I was momentarily confused. One minute, she was whispering for me not to go, then the very next minute, she was telling me that I had to go. I narrowed my eyes before finally realizing what she was doing. She was trying to warn me while still delivering the other covens' message.

"If what they want is a road to diplomacy, then they will accept my representative with open arms. It shouldn't matter if I don't appear in person."

"You were warned." A hint of a smile appeared on Natalie's face.

I nodded. "Warning taken. However, it's in my best interest to remain at The Shade for now."

Natalie nodded before a guard escorted her to one of the submarines that would lead her off the island and back to the mainland.

"What was that all about? Sending Gregor Novak to the meeting with the coven leaders?" Corrine asked.

I shook my head. "I'm just trying to protect Natalie. She's gotten herself into a lot of trouble because of me."

"Yes. Trouble. It seems to chase you wherever you go."

"I have no idea how to get to Sofia, Corrine, and if I leave The Shade, there's no telling what could happen. This place is in chaos. Felix and Gregor could easily take over...".

"Gregor is already detained at The Cells. He isn't going to cause you any trouble now."

"He's still my father, Corrine. I can't just keep him locked in there."

"I guess Sofia had more effect on you than I initially thought. I know the Novaks' loyalties to each other are very strong—it's what kept you alive so long—but the Derek legends speak of wouldn't have hesitated to destroy his own father. It's why you were so feared."

"Every day is a battle to keep the Derek legends speak of from emerging once again. I can't afford to be that person." *Sofia's hand clasping mine. Her smile. Her touch.* I ached for her so much it made it difficult to breathe. "If the other covens attack, I wouldn't know what to do. We could lose everything. There must be a way out of this. Do you think I should meet with the other coven leaders? Maybe it's not too late…"

"I think you should find Sofia, Derek. Prophecy is prophecy… You won't be able to fulfill your destiny unless she is by your side."

I knew full well that the only reason I'd survived being taken by the hunters was because of Sofia. Aiden had warned me that should I ever return, he wouldn't be as kind. Dread filled me at the thought of dying in the hunters' hands.

I caught sight of one of the guards coming out of the Port, recognizing him as one of Xavier's men usually stationed at The Cells. I called on him to give him instructions. "Let Ashley and Eli know that I want them to come to my penthouse first thing tomorrow. Tell them that we're going to locate hunter territory." Of all the people who could possibly help me narrow down the location of hunter headquarters, it was them. "Also, check if the lockdown has been ended."

"Of course, sir." The guard bowed before heading off.

"And what are *you* going to do until tomorrow?" Corrine asked from behind me.

"Sleep. I haven't had any of that since I arrived at The Shade. Come to think about it, I haven't had any blood either." I flashed Corrine a grin. "Perhaps that's the reason you look so enticing."

"Watch it, Novak. All it takes is one spell from me to end you."

I saw a hint of a smile on her twitching lip. I raised my hands in the air in mock surrender. "Some other woman has already cast a spell on me."

She nodded knowingly, this time a full smile appearing on her face. "The magic of Sofia Claremont."

I chuckled. No matter what happened, Sofia would always be a part of me. A mixture of sadness and affection came with the next thought: *Perhaps that's it. That's how we're going to be together. Sofia will forever be in my thoughts, in my soul, in my heart. Perhaps we don't have to be physically together.*

That night, for the first time since I had left her, I could no longer picture her face. I shut my eyes, holding on to whatever figments of her were left inside me. *No. I need to find you, Sofia. I can't let you slip away.*

CHAPTER 31: SOFIA

Ingrid Maslen was human and she wasn't happy about it. Aiden and I watched from surveillance monitors in another room as she tore at her cot's bedding and screamed her lungs out.

A guard dropped by to give her a plate of food and she looked at the sandwich as if it were the most despicable thing she'd ever laid eyes on. The tray and the meal were thrown straight against the wall.

"How could you do this to me?" she yelled into the camera.

"I guess the cure works," was all Aiden said.

I tilted my head, not knowing whether to be amused or elated or just bothered. "I think the cure works to rid the person of vampirism, but it doesn't work to cure them of their craziness."

"Did you really believe that she could be cured of that?"

"Don't tell me that you're not still hoping for the same thing."

All I got from my father was a bittersweet smile. That was

enough of an answer. I stood on my tiptoes to kiss him on the cheek. "Thank you for believing me."

His face tightened, his eyes once again fixed on the surveillance monitor, watching the woman he loved making a fool of herself.

"May I speak with her again?" I asked.

"Are you sure? It wouldn't come as a surprise if she attacks you."

"I think I can handle it. I'll be fully equipped." I tapped my thigh where I had a wooden stake and a UV ray gun inside a holster.

"She's no longer a vampire... The gun or even the stake, if not used well, could maim her."

I had to laugh at how overprotective he was being. "Maiming her is good enough to protect myself, I think."

"Before you go ahead and talk to her, how do you intend to get the cure to Derek?"

"I'd have to go back to The Shade." I shrugged. It seemed like the obvious answer.

"I'm not letting you go back there alone. What if the cure doesn't work and they keep you captive there?" His face took on a grim expression as he shook his head, and I could tell that there was no dissuading him from his doubts.

I swallowed hard. "Derek is never going to allow hunters into The Shade."

"I don't care if we have to meet him outside of that secret island kingdom of his. I'm going with you, Sofia. And that's that. I don't care how in love you are with this person, I can't lose my daughter again."

I understood where he was coming from, but I had no idea

how to communicate with Derek without going back to The Shade. *Unless...* "Well, there's this girl. Natalie Borgia. You know her?"

My father's brow rose.

"I'm sure either Claudia or Ingrid would know how to get in touch with her. We'd have to promise her safety. Messing with her is like messing with every single vampire out there, so..."

"I know how important she is," Aiden cut me off. "You can trust me. She won't be harmed."

I wanted to trust him, I really did, but staring up at him, I couldn't help but wonder how much of him was Aiden, my father, and how much of him was Reuben, the hunter. Still, I wanted to believe that he was sincere, that he was on my side. *Isn't he already getting heat from the higher-ups about his decisions lately?*

"I'll get the information we need from Ingrid or Claudia. I do have one condition..."

He narrowed his eyes at me. "What is it?"

"Claudia and Vivienne will be going with us. They deserve to get back home to The Shade. If they want the cure, then that's for them to decide, but I don't want them here any longer."

"Sofia, you have to realize the trouble I'm gonna get into if I just let them go... I'm already dealing with enough heat after letting Derek go."

"I know, but I'm not going to leave them here."

"Leave them? Sofia, you're talking like you're not coming back."

"Dad, I belong with Derek. If the cure works and he turns back into a human, then I owe it to myself and to him to actually give what we have a shot. We're engaged. If the cure works, we *are* going to get married."

His eyes darkened. Clearly, the idea of me marrying Derek Novak—vampire or not—wasn't something he was happy about.

"We'll discuss that in due time. You can have a talk with your mother now if you want."

I loved Aiden. He was my father, but this was my life. He couldn't stand in the way of what I had with Derek. This was something I was going to fight for.

At that moment, however, the fight I faced was with my mother, or perhaps the lingering affection I still held for her. I had no idea what to expect or why I even wanted to talk to her. Maybe I wanted to give her another chance.

She looked daggers my way the moment I entered her cell.

"I can't believe you would do this to me," she hissed.

I looked at her, a reflection of me. From the moment I first laid eyes on her, I'd always thought of her as more beautiful than I was. I sat on the cot—or at least what was left of it—as I stared at her.

"I don't understand," I mused as the cell doors closed, a guard watching nearby.

"Understand what, Sofia?"

"How you could turn your back on Aiden. I'm sure you loved him and he loved you. Why would you willingly become something that keeps you away from him?"

"You mean a vampire? Did you not choose to remain human even in spite of your love for Derek? Isn't that the same thing?"

"I didn't want to be turned into a vampire." I nodded. "But when I realized that it was perhaps the only way I could be with him, I *did* ask him to turn me—mostly to see if I would turn.

When I didn't, I was devastated to realize that I couldn't become what I needed to be in order to be with him."

"Exactly. I couldn't become what I needed to be in order to be with Aiden. I couldn't become Camilla. I couldn't become the perfect housewife. I was weak and afraid. Every day I was haunted by the thought that he might see me for the broken creature that I am and leave me. Especially in contrast to your perfection, how could I have stood a chance?"

"I am your daughter, Ingrid. I don't understand how you could see me as competition."

At that, she sealed her lips and I knew that my words had triggered dark memories that she dared not speak of.

"You don't know what you're saying," was all she said. "You and Aiden ruined me when you turned me back into a human. I was powerful and strong as a vampire. Now, I'm back to being what I was before: weak and mortal."

"At least now you and Aiden can have a chance at being together again."

"Not as long as you're alive." She raised her eyes to meet mine and I shuddered to find so much hatred in her gaze. "What are you seeking to accomplish with this cure, Sofia? You plan to turn Derek Novak back into a human so you can raise kids in a picket-fence house, live the American dream and frolic together in your own happily ever after? Don't be a fool, Sofia. You and Derek don't belong together."

"The same way you and my father don't?"

"Derek will only make you weak, Sofia. Just like your father did to me. Turned me back into a human, into this whimpering pathetic weakling... Borys will make you strong."

She curled up into the corner of the room, knees held to her chest as she fought back sobs. I approached her tentatively, wondering if she was still planning to attack me.

When I sat in front of her, she shied away from me, but it wasn't like she had any space to back into. I brushed a hand over her long auburn locks and she flinched at my touch. I kissed her forehead and was surprised at how she trembled.

"You might be surprised at how powerful a force love is, Mother." I pressed my lips against her cheek, realizing that this might be the last kiss I gave her. "For all it's worth, I do love you, Camilla."

She glared at me, but I meant what I had said. I backed away from her and signaled for the guard to let me out. As I took a turn toward the hallway that would lead me out of the hawk headquarters' dungeons, I could swear that I heard Ingrid Maslen sob.

Chapter 32: Derek

Things were getting back to normal—or at least it seemed that way. After we heard their demands, we told the humans that we would look into their requests and see that their living conditions were improved. With that settled, the humans were back at their posts. We were still hunting down Felix and the few men who still remained with him. Those who surrendered had been given amnesty in exchange for their loyalty.

The only remaining threat was the attack of the covens—which we hadn't heard from Natalie about.

"What if they agree to you sending Gregor?" Ashley asked. "I don't understand why you would send him in your stead."

We were at my penthouse's dining room with Eli, who had just stepped out to get us some blood when Ashley broached the subject of the meeting with the coven leaders.

"Trust me. They won't. They're bent on declaring war on The

Shade. Of that, I am sure. I won't be surprised if my father's working with them."

"It seems like a dangerous assumption to risk the entire island on."

"I just know. I know, Natalie. I could tell by the way she was acting. They're going to declare war on us whether I go or not, and if there's war, I think we all stand a better chance if I'm here at The Shade."

"Then what about looking for Sofia?"

I inwardly groaned. We'd been discussing everything we knew about the hunters and we'd narrowed down our search for their headquarters to a certain spot on the map.

We had information that witches still worked for the hunters. Headquarters could be hidden by a spell the same way The Shade was.

"I want more than anything to have Sofia back here, but maybe we're wasting our time with all this... Maybe this is how it's supposed to be."

Ashley gave me a smack on the shoulder. "I can't believe you! We're at this again? Really? I know Sofia. The fact that you left her there is probably driving her insane! How could you do that to her? I don't care how you think it's supposed to be. Sofia belongs here with you and not out there as some sort of spoiled, rich princess to her father, the lord of the hunters."

Eli stepped into the dining room, glasses of blood in hand. He began placing the glasses on the table in front of us. "What's going on?"

"Do you think Derek should leave here and look for Sofia as soon as possible?" Ashley asked.

Eli took a sip from his glass of blood. "I suppose, but I'm not sure about 'as soon as possible.'" He directed his attention toward me. "I understand how important Sofia is, but I can't help but feel as if we're wasting time looking for her when there's an imminent attack on The Shade. Should we not be fortifying our defenses and gearing up for war?"

I cast a triumphant look at Ashley, who sent death glares at Eli.

Truth be told, my heart sank. Though my brain was telling me the same things Eli was saying, deep inside, I was desperate to find Sofia—whether it was because of my love for her or my craving for her blood, I was no longer sure.

A knock on the front door interrupted our conversation. I stood up to answer it despite Eli's offer to get the door. I walked up to the front door and swung it open to find Xavier and Natalie standing at my doorstep.

"Look who's back," Xavier announced. "Apparently, she can't get enough of the chaos."

"Or maybe she just misses you." I shrugged.

Natalie stepped forward, giving Xavier a glare. She set her eyes on me. "You're going to need a seat for what I'm about to tell you."

I swallowed hard and waved toward my living room. Natalie seemed to be bracing herself for what she had to say. "I have two messages. One is from the vampire covens. The other is from Sofia Claremont. Which one do you want to hear first?"

I froze. I knew what to expect from the vampire covens. I had no idea what Sofia's message would be. The unknown seemed a lot more fearsome than the immense threat that came with the known. "I'd like to hear what the other vampire covens have to say."

Natalie cleared her throat. "Their message is simple. Three words. 'Prepare for war.'"

"They sent you all the way here just to say that?" Xavier grimaced.

I straightened up in my seat and nodded. "Very well then. All I can say is another three words. 'Let them come.'" I paused, surprised that war—something I'd feared would happen—wasn't alarming me as much as it should have. Knowing that Sofia had me in mind rattled me more. "The second message?"

"Understand that there was no way for me to meet with her. It was too dangerous to see her personally, with her being in the hunters' hands, so we had to communicate by phone."

I understood the implication. If Natalie was somehow bugged by the other covens, then they had most likely heard what Sofia had said.

"Sofia says that she might have found a way for you and her to be together. She wants to meet with you at a hotel in Cancún." Natalie handed me a small note. "Those are the details of the time and place."

I took the note and drew a breath at what was written: *They know the time and place. It's too dangerous. Sofia is talking about a cure to vampirism.*

It felt like a rock lodged itself in my throat as I read the last phrase over and over and over again. *A cure to vampirism.* Not once since I had turned into a vampire had it ever even crossed my mind that there could be a cure. *How is that possible?*

A cure. A cure! If I turned back into a human, I would be mortal. Sofia and I could get married, have children, grow old together... The deepest desires of my heart made possible.

Hope unlike anything I'd felt before surged within me. *Could she have really done it? Could she really have found a way for us to be together?*

"Well?" Natalie broke the tense silence, her eyes set on the piece of paper she had handed over to me. I was shaking as I held it in my hand. "What do you want me to tell her?"

"Tell her to come to The Shade. I can't risk leaving. Not with an impending war. If I'm going to meet with her, then it would have to be here."

"You do realize that she doesn't plan to meet with you alone, right? The hunters will be with her—most likely her own father."

"Derek..." Xavier was shaking his head, clearly about to object. "I know how much Sofia matters to you, but for crying out loud... she's with the hunters. Is now really the best time to accommodate hunters here at the island? We can barely keep things together."

A thousand possibilities crossed my mind all at once. Threatening. Overwhelming. Disturbing. I shook the thoughts out. There was no point in succumbing to the fears. "I need Sofia to find true sanctuary. The prophecy makes that clear. If the only way she can get back here is with the hunters, then so be it. Let them come. Let them *all* come."

If war has to happen, I can't stop it. I just know that I need Sofia by my side. If this is the only way, then so be it.

CHAPTER 33: CLAUDIA

I was their gift to him.

Yuri was celebrating his twenty-first birthday and his newfound friends wanted to give him a woman. The Duke decided that I would be perfect for the young man who was already being acclaimed as an artist of great genius. Of course, my master also knew that Yuri meant so much more to me than that.

When I was presented to Yuri, I could tell that he was uncomfortable with the idea. I'd seen the same look in his eyes with countless other men before him. Still, it never stopped them.

Both of us were practically shoved into a room, with hoots and cheers for Yuri to enjoy himself. I stood there trembling. I often shook before the Duke, but in front of Yuri, it was for very different reasons. With Yuri, I'd never felt more vulnerable than I did at that moment.

"Could you please take off the mask?" he asked.

"I can't. I'm not allowed to." I hoped that he wouldn't recognize

my voice. I hoped that I would never have to reveal myself to him, but I also understood why the Duke had instructed me not to remove it until Yuri was finished with me. The Duke relished the idea of Yuri finding out that he'd been pursuing a whore. I swallowed back the tears.

He approached me and raised his hand. I flinched from his touch, afraid that he would take the mask off. Instead, he just brushed a thumb over my exposed collarbone, the flimsy dress I was wearing leaving little to his imagination.

"Should we begin?" I asked, motioning to get on the bed. I half-expected him to stop me, to tell me that this didn't feel right, considering he was pursuing another woman. I wanted to believe that he was a decent man, but I should've known that he was what he was: a man.

As I lay down on the bed, my heart broke when he climbed on top of me and began gently undoing the laces on the bodice of my gown. As he did what he came there to do, I tried to shut my mind off. I tried to think of him as someone other than the young man who'd courted me over the past weeks, but I couldn't. Yuri was just like every other man: out to use women like me.

When he was done, his weight fell atop me and without asking me, he removed the mask. I didn't have the will to resist. At that point, I didn't care anymore if he saw me for what I was, because I saw him for what he was too.

When our eyes met, I barely recognized him through the blur of my own tears. Despite the haziness, however, I still made out the shock in his eyes.

"It's you." He got off me and pulled his clothes back on in a hurry. I tried to show him that I was strong, that my heart wasn't

breaking, but my resolve was crumbling. I sat up and took my place on the edge of the bed, trying not to cry as I pulled my dress back on. I wanted to get out of that room, but I was shaking so badly, I could barely get the dress on.

His face softened as he watched me struggle. I couldn't decipher the expression on his face.

Is he disgusted by me? Does he think less of me now than he did before?

"Stop," he ordered me after I failed once again to get my arms through the sleeves of the dress.

By pure instinct, I heeded his command. That was the training the Duke had put me through. Every order was followed immediately and without question. I dropped my arms to my sides, allowing the top of the dress to fall over the bunched skirt of the outfit.

Yuri approached me and held my arms, coaxing me to stand up. Afraid that the skirt would fall to the ground and expose me, I hung on to the dress, holding it just below my waist as I let him study me.

I didn't dare look at his face as he perused me, but I sensed it when he swallowed hard. "Why do you have so many bruises?"

Why does it matter? *As usual, I didn't respond. In my book, he didn't deserve a response. Not after he had just used me.*

"Who did this to you? Is this why I can't walk with you anymore? Is this why you wouldn't accept even the smallest of gifts from me?"

I hated his questions. I didn't want to have to answer them. After all, what was the point? The charade we'd had was over. "Is there anything else you would have me do for you?"

"Yes. Answer my questions and tell me your name."

"I can't do that."

"Can't or won't?"

"Both."

The silence was so deafening, I finally managed to look up at him. I was surprised, because what I saw was something I'd never seen from the Duke. Guilt.

"I'm so sorry," he told me.

I couldn't fight back the urge to scoff at him. "You're sorry? Would you have been sorry if you had never seen who was behind the mask?"

He gulped. "I was sorry even while I was… while we were… This is wrong. I never should've gone along with this."

"Then why did you?" Why does anyone? Do they have any idea how much ruin they bring to us?

He didn't respond. Instead, he lifted the bodice of my gown over my body and began lacing it up. "This time, I really do understand," he said. "Nothing has changed. In my eyes, you're still the beautiful woman in the woods, the same one I wouldn't mind taking a walk with every day for the rest of my life, the same one who enthralled me from the first moment I laid my eyes on her."

He kissed my lips—the most tender and precious kiss I'd ever experienced.

"I'm sorry I did this to you. I'm sorry you have to go through this, but know that I will spend my whole life making it up to you. I swear it."

He was true to his word. I didn't think Yuri ever forgave himself for sleeping with me that night. In fact, even when I made advances on him over the past centuries, he never responded.

He was the one who'd turned me into a vampire. He'd done it so I could protect myself from the Duke. Yuri had protected me for hundreds of years.

I hated it when he was with any other woman and I knew that

he hated it whenever I was with any other man, but that was the way it'd always been with Yuri. We couldn't stand being apart, but somehow, we both knew that we couldn't be together either. I'd asked him once why that was and his answer was blunt. "I want to be with you, Claudia. I think you know that, but I don't think you'll ever enjoy us being together until you get that sixteen-year-old victim out of you."

That was the day I realized that Yuri saw right through me. I knew that he didn't care about my past, that he would accept me if only I could accept myself. He also knew that I would find it difficult to forgive him for sleeping with me that night. Until I was ready, until I could let go of my past, we could never be together.

When I left The Shade, that was exactly what had happened to me.

I'd realized that the past didn't matter, that I'd been wasting my immortality being so caught up in avenging my past against someone I had already ended. I'd been punishing both Yuri and myself for a past neither of us could ever change.

What I would do to take it all back and do things differently...

The door creaked open and Sofia emerged. I hadn't heard from Sofia since she had told me that she was going to escape.

"Sofia!" I jumped out of the bed to greet her. "Were you able to do it? Were you able to find a way to escape to The Shade? And now you've come back for me?"

She shook her head and gave me a soft smile. "I got caught. You really can't trust some people."

My heart sank. I breathed out a sigh and shrugged. "I guess this is it then. I deserve this fate. My fault for being so stupid all these years."

I couldn't have predicted what Sofia was going to say next in a million years, but when she said it, it was music to my ears.

"No, Claudia. We're going back to The Shade."

Chapter 34: Ingrid

My daughter was a relentless plague I couldn't seem to get rid of. Her words cut like a knife and kept cutting.

You might be surprised at how powerful a force love is, Mother.

Mother. She'd called me Mother. She'd told me she loved me.

Naïve young woman. I scoffed even as I sat on that wretched cot inside that wretched dungeon, lamenting my humanity. However, as much as I hated to admit it, deep inside, I knew the truth. She was stronger in spirit and more powerful in her kindness than I could ever be. Sofia was everything I was not, everything I wished I could be. Perhaps that was why I loathed her so much.

I couldn't understand how she could be so strong even clothed in her frail humanity. When I'd realized what Aiden had done, that he had exacted the ultimate punishment upon me by turning me back into a human being, it had torn me apart. It felt like losing everything that had made me who I was. I'd lashed out.

When Sofia had visited me, she'd come as a wave of calm in the storm I was brewing up. I'd taken one look at her—beautiful and brave—and known that there was something deeply wrong with me for envying her.

I was still musing over her words when Aiden showed up.

"How could you do this to me?" I glared at him.

He just stepped in. The bars behind him shut closed and we were left alone.

I tried to hold my glare at him as he stared right back. It was a battle of wills I couldn't win. I shuddered as I looked into his green eyes, butterflies fluttering in my stomach—a sensation I hadn't felt since I turned into a vampire. I couldn't help but break the stare as I bowed my head, my eyes downcast. "What do you want from me, Aiden?"

"Can you never be Camilla again?"

"Isn't that what you've turned me into? Am I not once again human? Weak and vulnerable to your every advance? Pining for you? Unworthy of you?"

"Is that what you felt all those years we were together, Camilla? That you were unworthy? That you were weak?"

How could he not know that that was exactly how I had felt? More than that, I couldn't believe that he had called me by that name again. *Camilla.* I couldn't understand it, but my heart leaped.

"I never saw you that way. You were vibrant and strong-willed and adventurous. You were sweet and kind. You were beautiful in every way as Camilla Claremont, and then you became Ingrid Maslen and now look at you…"

His words stung. All these years, I'd looked down on Camilla.

To be told that he found her beautiful was daunting to me.

"What do you want from me, Aiden? I'm human now. Shouldn't I be released from this prison by now? Or do you torment and brainwash humans too?"

Aiden shook his head slowly. "What do I want from you? I just wanted you to know that what you wanted—Sofia belonging to your beloved lord, Borys... it's not going to happen. We're about to turn Derek Novak into a human being—just like you—and there's nothing you can do about it."

Those words made me livid, reinforcing that a part of Ingrid Maslen still remained with me. "She belongs with Borys Maslen!" I screamed at him.

Sadness unlike anything I had ever seen before filled his eyes. "I wish you wouldn't say that. I guess human or not, you will always be Ingrid Maslen. Goodbye."

Left to myself, I felt the hopelessness of my defeat. It felt like Sofia had won. I had nothing left. Sofia, on the other hand, was about to get everything she had ever wanted. It didn't seem fair.

Why live to see her celebrating her triumph over me?

Desperate, I took a shard of glass left over from a glass of water I'd thrown against the wall. I tried to recall the last time I had felt pain as a human. Horrible memories I had long buried flashed through my mind, reminding me how cruel humans could be, how cold-hearted and merciless they were. *I don't want to be among them.* I slashed the glass across my wrist, wincing at the pain.

I waited. Blood gushed out of my wrist. I was expecting to immediately sense the call of death upon me, but nothing happened. The blood just kept trickling until to my shock, the gash on my wrist began to close.

I stared at my wrist in horror. *What's going on?* I slashed the knife through my skin again—this time a deeper, more lethal gash. Within minutes, the same thing happened.

I had no idea what was going on, but one thing seemed true.

I was still immortal.

CHAPTER 35: DEREK

Word of the hunters coming to the island spread like wildfire. As was expected, reactions were mostly negative. The vampires who remained neutral were beginning to question my sanity. Those who were loyal, on the other hand, voiced their concerns. While some were quick to assure me that I had their support, I knew that their trust in me was wavering.

The arrival of the hunters seemed to spark hope of an escape from The Shade among some of the Naturals. Gavin and Ian explained to them that hunters didn't exactly see humans taken captives by vampires as worth saving. The human slaves of The Oasis had been massacred right along with their vampire lords. This knowledge didn't quell their hopes.

I was questioning my own judgment, but I knew Sofia, and I knew that she would not suggest something she believed could bring The Shade harm. *Unless of course they've gotten to her somehow and turned her against me...*

"Am I making the right decision?" I asked Corrine, having found my way to her home—The Sanctuary.

She stared at me warily. We both knew that my coming to her for advice was completely out of character. Still, she gave me a piece of her mind. "I think you're doing what you need to do in order to get Sofia back here. That's what's important."

"Is it really possible that there's a cure?" I asked the witch. "You know these things."

She paused, seeming to access a distant memory as she wrinkled her nose in thought. "There were attempts to find a cure before, but I haven't heard of any successful ones. I wouldn't even really call it a 'cure.' Vampirism, as we know it, is a curse, not a disease."

"I don't think Sofia would propose something this big unless she believes it will work."

"I don't doubt Sofia." Corrine nodded. "I'm curious too."

"Perhaps it has something to do with her being the immune..." My eyes sparked with interest. "Maybe she has somehow become the antidote."

"The immune?" Corrine narrowed her eyes at me and I realized that since my arrival at The Shade, I hadn't told anyone about Sofia being immune.

"Claudia tried to turn Sofia. And at Sofia's request, back at hunter territory, so did I... She didn't turn."

Corrine's brows furrowed with confusion. "I didn't think... Oh, wow..."

"What?"

"Well, I thought it was a myth that there are immunes. Somehow immunes survive the three days that follow after being bitten. Legend says that if the immune doesn't die or turn in those three days, they disappear. Or they go crazy. It's because their senses and emotions are heightened. Their human mind is unable to cope with this and they snap... I didn't think it was true. My mother always told me it was an old wives' tale..."

"Maybe that's why Sofia was exhibiting signs of that psychological disorder you diagnosed her with," I mused. "What was that again? LLI?"

"Low Latent Inhibition." Corrine nodded.

"Wait. You mean there are more out there like Sofia?"

"If the legend is true, yes, but so far, Sofia's the only one I've ever heard of."

I frowned, remembering one insane person at The Shade. "Maybe she isn't the only one..."

"What do you mean?"

"Didn't Felix want to turn Anna before? That's what I was told..."

Corrine's brown eyes narrowed. "He wanted to, yes, but there's no indication that he ever tried to turn her. That's what was so surprising about it. He was in love with her one minute, wanting to turn her and be with her forever, and then he just abandoned her. When he left her at The Catacombs, she was already insane."

"What if he actually did try to turn her? Perhaps he really did want to be with her, and she didn't turn."

"You think Anna is an immune too?"

"Don't you think it's possible?"

The witch's eyes lit up. "It does seem like a possibility. It could even explain why she went crazy. If you're right about Sofia exhibiting the signs of LLI because of the fact that she wasn't turned, perhaps Anna wasn't able to handle it the way Sofia was able to. Still, the only person who could verify that is Felix." Corrine shrugged. "He would be the only one who would know if he had ever tried to turn her. Heaven knows we can't get any trustworthy information from Anna."

I grimaced, remembering why I was so distraught in the first place. I was to meet with Felix and his men for negotiations with the humans. I had no idea how Eli and Yuri had managed to find Felix, much less convince the man to talk with me, and I wasn't exactly looking forward to the meeting—one that, for some reason, they had decided to hold at the Port—apparently Felix's "neutral ground."

"Wish me luck," I told Corrine before leaving for the Port.

A couple minutes later, I was fighting to hold myself back from ripping several hearts out.

All of them. They're going to drive me insane.

"I'm not going to work with the humans," Felix repeated, shaking his head.

"It's not like we want to work with you," Ian shot back.

"You're here to work for me, boy, not with me." Felix glared at me. "See what you've done? You've let these weaklings entertain the delusion that they are our equals."

"This island will crumble without us." Ian was now on his feet, his nostrils flaring as he boldly stood up against a creature that could easily break his neck in two.

My jaw tightened as I tried to reel in my frustration. It seemed Felix and his men had had no idea what the word 'negotiation' meant when they had agreed to the meeting. They had it in their heads that they were there to make demands. I was trying to drive home the point that if we didn't come together, the other covens were going to annihilate everything we'd worked to establish over the past years. None of this fazed Felix, who was adamant that he would never lower himself to work with humans. They were supposed to be his slaves.

At some point, Ian must've had enough of Felix, because he ignored the man and set his attention on me. "You know I'm with you in this, Derek, but not all the humans are willing to fight in this battle. Most of the humans want to just sit this whole thing out. Others are hoping to escape during the heat of the battle."

I couldn't blame the humans for saving themselves. The other covens had their sights set on The Shade, but it seemed it was going to implode before they even stepped ashore.

I was hoping that this meeting could help us arrive at some sort of compromise before Sofia, Aiden and the hunters they'd brought with them arrived. Of course, it seemed the negotiations weren't going to lead to an actual resolution.

"Who cares about the humans we already have here? They're easy to replace." Felix brushed Ian's announcement off.

"You mean the same way you brushed Anna off?" Ian hissed.

Felix responded with a wide grin. "Ah, Anna. Word is you have an eye for my little pet. How is she, that lovely one?"

Ian was obviously using his own self-control not to attack. I, on the other hand, voiced my own thoughts about Anna. "You were in love with Anna once, were you not?"

Felix raised a brow at me. "Perhaps. What's that to you?"

"She was human."

"She was a freak."

"A freak?" I sat up straight. "How so? Rumors were you wanted to turn her into one of us so that you could be with her forever. You used to worship the ground she walked on, then suddenly, you just didn't want her anymore?"

Felix gulped. His jaw tightened.

"What did you do to her?" Ian hissed.

The tone of accusation made Felix's temper flare. "I did nothing to her. She was supposed to be mine. We were supposed to be together, but no matter what I did, she wouldn't turn into one of us. She remained human until she just went insane... Happy now? Is that what you wanted to hear?"

I tried to hide the smile. "I know why she didn't turn. It's the same reason Sofia didn't. They're both immune."

Felix narrowed his eyes at me. "What does that even mean?"

I shook my head. "It doesn't matter. It's not why we're here. Bottom line, Felix, is whether or not you will work with us."

Stubborn as a mule, the man shook his head. "You're going to run this kingdom into the ground, Derek. With rumors going on that you're about to allow hunters into The Shade..."

"That's none of your business," was all I told him. The thought made my heart leap. *Sofia is coming with a cure.* It seemed too good to be true, but it was the one thing that I was hanging all my hopes on at that moment.

We weren't going to accomplish anything that day. Felix was too obstinate and Ian was just a boy who didn't hold any sway when it came to the majority of the masses occupying The Catacombs.

The reality that we were about to go to war while still fighting amongst ourselves was sinking in. *Unless Sofia's cure actually works...* A cure would change life as I knew it. *It would change everything.*

"Are you even listening to what we're saying?" Felix slammed a fist on the table between us.

I glared at him. "I ask you one final time, Felix. Will you work with us or not?"

"No. Never."

"Then why on earth would I listen to you?" I stood to my feet and spoke into the communication device Eli had given me before the meeting. "Have them all arrested. I don't want them causing any trouble."

At that, Felix broke into a huge grin. "I knew I couldn't trust you, so before we came here, I made sure I had a safeguard. If I don't come out of the Port alive and free, I have a man waiting by the chilling chambers ready to set the chambers—and all the blood supply this island has—on fire. With all your people starving for blood, let's see you try to keep these human pests safe."

Ian's eyes grew wide with shock. "You sick bastard..."

"What's to say you won't destroy the chambers even if I let you go?"

"Well, you'll just have to trust me, Novak."

Anger was taking over me and I could sense the darkness coming. If Felix made good on his threat to destroy the chambers, any progress I had made in quelling a human revolt would be gone. Any loyalties the vampires had toward me would certainly be placed on shaky ground.

I snapped. I couldn't fight the rage anymore. Before I could stop myself, I had his neck wrapped in my fingers and I blacked out. In my last moment of sanity, I tried to remember Sofia's face,

Sofia's touch, but when I did, all I felt was a deep hunger, an immense craving for her blood that only served to inch me further toward darkness.

Power filled me as I ripped Felix's heart out. Barely a minute later, there was a loud explosion and I knew then that I'd just signed up for more destruction than I knew how to handle.

Still squeezing Felix's beating heart in my hand, I stood to my full height and raised my eyes. My blood started pounding, because right there in front of me, with her mouth agape, stood Sofia.

I dropped the heart on the ground. I wanted to take her in my arms, breathe in her scent, feel her body against mine, hear her words, touch her… but more than that, I wanted to sink my teeth into her neck and drink. Drink deep.

I can't live without her and yet I can't be with her either.

Sofia Claremont is going to lead me to my ruin.

Confused, I did the only thing I could do to keep Sofia safe. I ran.

My heart ached when she softly whispered my name.

"Derek, I love you."

Chapter 36: Sofia

I stood frozen as I watched Derek leave.

My father stood right beside me. I knew that he had seen what I had seen even though I'd got to the Port ahead of him. I couldn't even begin to fathom what was going through his mind—especially when Derek took one look at me and bolted.

This was nothing like the reunion I'd had in mind. I hadn't even realized how much I was pining for Derek until I stood there, rooted to my spot, not knowing how to process the emotions coursing through me.

Xavier and Ian remained with us—along with Sam and Kyle, who had fetched us from the shore and taken us to the island. Xavier and Ian exchanged uncomfortable glances before nodding my way.

"This is awkward," Ian muttered. "But it's great to see you again, Sofia." He hesitated before approaching me and giving me a short hug. "It's been crazy here since you left," he whispered in my ear, before stepping away from me and giving Aiden a short glance.

Xavier scratched his head. "Welcome back to all this chaos, Sofia. You'll find that The Shade is not the same as it was when you left. I'm assuming this"—he eyed Aiden—"is your father, the infamous Reuben... Was he told that the humans who come into The Shade never leave?"

I knew that he was trying to lighten a tense situation, but the joke fell flat—especially when Aiden's nostrils flared at the slightest notion of him being imprisoned there.

"Relax, Dad," I told him. "He's joking." I turned to Xavier. "There's someone back at the sub whom I know you'd love to see again. She needs her rest and she's not exactly in perfect shape, but Vivienne is..."

He didn't even wait for me to finish. He was out of there and running to the submarine the moment her name escaped my lips.

"Look who's back," Sam said, with not a single hint of enthusiasm in his tone.

Claudia had just emerged from the submarine. She rolled her eyes at Sam, never being one to bother with those she perceived as lesser than her. Still, when the lowly guard was the only one who acknowledged her presence, she heaved a sigh and asked him anyway. "How's Yuri?"

Sam frowned in surprise. "Fine, I guess."

Right about then, a familiar face appeared from the entrance to the Port. I couldn't help but squeal with delight at the sight of her. "Ashley!"

She responded in kind, shouting my name out as we embraced

each other. Despite everything we'd been through at The Shade and despite the fact that she was now an immortal vampire, the two of us were still teenagers, unafraid to express our delight upon seeing a long-lost friend.

"Sam told me you were coming today," she said enthusiastically as she squeezed me tight.

"Ow," I complained. "You're a vampire now. You're stronger than you were before."

"Oops." She pulled away from me and grimaced. "Sorry. I still forget sometimes. I was planning to hang out here at the Port to wait for you, but Felix had to choose the Port as the place to hold his negotiations with Derek." She wrinkled her nose. "Where is he anyway?"

"He bolted the moment he saw me. We arrived just in time to see him do *that*." I pointed at Felix's heartless body on the ground.

Ashley eyed the corpse. "I think we need someone to get this mess fixed up."

"Kyle's on it," Sam assured her.

I couldn't help but notice the way their eyes lingered on each other's before Ashley blushed and looked away.

Aiden cleared his throat to make his presence—largely ignored—known.

"Sorry... Ashley, this is my father, Aiden Claremont. This is Ashley. She's one of my dearest friends here."

Ashley extended her hand for Aiden to shake, but he just stared at it. "You're a vampire too."

Ashley nervously began fumbling with her fingers. "Yes, sir. I'm the youngest vampire here at The Shade, so I'm also probably the easiest one to kill..." She furrowed her brows as if wondering to

herself why she had just said that. "I used to be a hunter too…
Well, I wasn't a very good one…"

"Yes. I thought you looked familiar."

Right about then, Xavier emerged, carrying a frail Vivienne in
his arms, her head against his broad shoulder. A flash of anger
shone through his eyes as he caught sight of Aiden.

"I'm taking her home," he announced. "You can stay here and
wait for Derek to get some self-control, or you can come with
me." He gave Aiden a glare. "I'm not sure Derek wants him on the
island."

"He's fine, Xavier. What can he do to anyone while he's here?"

"You're responsible for him, Sofia."

I nodded before daring to take a glimpse at my father. He had a
grim expression on his face. He hated being talked about like he
wasn't even present.

"What are we going to do with her?" Sam asked, eyeing
Claudia warily.

"Take her to The Cells." Xavier shrugged. "I don't really care."

"No." I shook my head. "She can come with me for now."

Xavier seemed surprised, but didn't bother to object. He just
went ahead to Vivienne's penthouse and we followed soon after.

My father walked beside me, silently taking in the darkness of
The Shade, not breathing a word. Ashley, on the other hand,
chattered nonstop, updating me on what had been going on at
The Shade. Sam and Claudia trailed behind us, the latter looking
like a lost little girl pining for home. I kept glancing back to check
on her. I noticed how she looked at all the vampires we passed,
almost as if she were wishing each of them would somehow morph
into Yuri.

"Do you have any idea where Yuri is?" I asked Ashley.

She shrugged. "The last time I saw him was when we quelled the siege at the Port. He keeps mostly to himself and only comes out when Derek calls for him." She looked back at Claudia. "What's up with her?"

"She's in love with Yuri," I told Ashley.

At this, the blonde cheerleader-turned-vampire raised a brow. "Wow. That's new. Claudia actually caring for someone other than herself…"

"I don't think she realized it until she was away from him. He'd always been there for her through the years. She took that for granted."

"Silly girl," Ashley muttered under her breath.

"I remember now."

I practically jumped out of my skin when Aiden spoke up. I glanced up at him and realized that he was looking at Ashley as we continued to walk past the giant redwoods.

"What?" I asked my dad.

"Ashley… You were the daughter of James and Helen. Your mother used to say that a lot about you: 'Silly girl.'"

Despite the dimness of our surroundings, lit up only by the light of the moon and the incandescent lighting that lined the pathways, I could tell that Ashley blushed at the reminder of her parents.

"My mother always thought that I was stupid for not wanting to join in their cause and become a hunter."

"Your father would go ballistic if he ever found out that you'd become a vampire. Do you have any idea how rattled they were when you disappeared?"

"I think you and I both know that I would've made a lousy hunter," Ashley responded, sounding a bit choked.

"Maybe so, but that doesn't mean that you can just go ahead and become the enemy."

"The enemy? Remember where you are, Reuben. You don't say things like that and expect to get out alive."

Aiden raised a brow at Ashley. "Is that a threat, girl?"

At that, Ashley chuckled. "I would never dare threaten you, Reuben. Vampire or not, I have no delusions of ever winning a fight with you. I do give you a friendly warning. Be careful, Reuben. Stay here long enough and you just might end up turning into one of us."

Before my father could respond, his eyes widened and his jaw slightly dropped. We'd just reached the Residences and for all the time I'd spent at The Shade, I'd forgotten how gorgeous the lavish villas constructed on top of the giant trees were. Around us a bustling community of vampires went about their business.

"This is incredible." Aiden mouthed the first—and perhaps last—compliment he'd given to a community of vampires. "We've attacked many covens before and I thought The Oasis was the most impressive, but this... I've never seen anything like this."

"They did well for themselves and for their kind, these Novaks." Ashley nodded. "Welcome to The Shade, Mr. Claremont."

Aiden began walking ahead of us and Ashley took the opportunity to link arms with me. She whispered to my ear, "I don't trust him. Reuben is famous for his hatred of vampires. I think he inherited the loathing from his family. It was in his bloodline, until.... Well, *you* came along." Ashley eyed Aiden warily. "I know he's your father, Sofia, but I know his kind. A leopard doesn't change its spots. He's not here to help you cure Derek or anyone else. What does that even mean?"

I wanted to explain to Ashley that I'd seen Ingrid be cured, that the cure was possible, that it was my idea, but I couldn't silence my own suspicions about Aiden's presence at The Shade either. All I could say was, "I don't fully trust him either, Ash."

"Then why risk us all by bringing him here, Sofia? If he ever finds a way to get the hunters here, we're all done for... especially considering that the other vampire covens have already declared war on Derek."

I shrugged, voicing my own hopes for the first time. "I guess I was hoping that by being here, he could see what we saw here at The Shade."

Ashley stopped in her tracks. "And what exactly do we see here?"

"Hope."

CHAPTER 37: DEREK

She's here.

I wanted nothing more than to hold her in my arms, but the urge to sink my teeth into the soft skin on her neck had become unbearable the moment I'd laid eyes on her. As if it weren't enough that she had come just in time to see me rip Felix's heart out, I couldn't risk spending the first few minutes of our reunion drinking her sweet blood. Still, even as I ran from her, I was keenly aware of how close she was, of how easy it would be for me to just take what I wanted from her.

No one could stop me. That was what scared me so much. Thus, I made my way to the one place with enough power to keep me from harming Sofia.

The Sanctuary.

"Back so soon? Since when can't you get enough of my company?" Corrine watched me, unfazed by the fact that I'd just barged into her study unannounced.

"Sofia is back. She returned with her father and I don't know who else." I sank onto one of the couches inside her study, my head down. "She returned right after Felix and his men blew up the chilling chambers and I lost it… I blacked out and I ripped Felix's heart out."

"The darkness took over?"

"I don't know what to do, Corrine."

"What do you mean you don't know what to do, Derek?" Corrine snapped. "Your fiancée has just returned. You go to her and you kiss her and you make her feel like she matters. What on earth are you doing here with me?"

"Don't you think I want to do that? After all the time we've been apart?" I ran a hand through my hair. "I want nothing more than to be with her, Corrine, but did you not hear me? The chilling chambers are gone… along with the blood. There's no blood left—apart from the human beings and animals at The Shade. How on earth am I going to control my craving for Sofia?"

"Well, you're certainly not going to be able to control it while ranting at me here, Derek. You have to face her and figure it out. One thing's for sure… you can't keep running away from her."

"You're no help at all. Don't you have any spell to help quench the craving?" I felt like a child throwing a tantrum as I crossed my arms over my chest.

"Didn't Sofia arrive saying that she and the hunters have found a cure? If you let her father administer the cure, then you won't have to come here asking for a spell, sulking like a little boy."

"Cora would've given me a spell—if one existed. I know she would've."

"I'm not Cora. Besides, she was in love with you. You could've asked her to jump off the walls of the Crimson Fortress and she would've done it. There's only one person on this island who would do the same thing for you and that's Sofia."

"Come with me. Please." I stood, intending to drag her all the way to my penthouse if I had to.

"What? No!"

"Don't you want to see Sofia? You two are good friends. If you're there, at least I'll know that someone is powerful enough to stop me in case I black out and…" I grabbed Corrine's wrist and gasped when she withdrew her hand and slapped me across my face.

"Pull yourself together, Novak. Sofia Claremont is far stronger than you give her credit for. Man up and give her the welcome she deserves."

Corrine was right. I was acting foolishly, but I couldn't help it. I was terrified of what I was capable of doing. "How could I ever forgive myself if I cause her more pain than I already have?"

"The same way you forgave yourself all those other times you made her miserable, Novak. You ask for her forgiveness and when you find that she loves you enough to see past what you've done, that's when you'll forgive yourself."

I was about to say something else, but the witch's brown eyes widened, and I shrank away from her.

"Get out of my sight, Novak."

I left The Sanctuary and took a long walk, my thirst for Sofia's blood not dwindling for a moment. I knew I had to face her eventually, and I knew that I had to exercise some form of control—if only to prove to Aiden that his daughter wasn't in danger around me.

I eventually ended up in my penthouse. Based on the level of thirst I had, she was nearby. I swallowed hard as I stepped into my living room, surprised to find Xavier there. He rose upon seeing me, fists clenched, the expression on his face indicating that he was just about ready to break someone's neck.

"You don't look very happy," was all I could think to say.

"Have you seen her?"

"Barely. You were there when she came… I couldn't stand being in the same room with her." I could practically hear her heartbeat, pumping blood into her veins, blood that would be pure ecstasy to me. "What I would give to—"

"Not Sofia. Vivienne."

My gut clenched and I took a step forward. "Don't mess with me, Xavier."

"She's alive. I'm not messing with you. She came with Sofia and her father. Claudia's with them too." Xavier shook his head. "She's not looking well."

"Where is she?" I hissed. Vivienne couldn't possibly be alive. No vampire had ever survived after being taken captive by the hunters. *Except me, and now there's Claudia… and Vivienne? How is this possible?*

"In her bedroom, but so is…"

I knew the warning he was about to give me. Sofia would be there, I had no doubt about it, but I didn't care. My twin was alive. *Vivienne survived.*

At that moment, that was all that mattered to me as I sped toward her penthouse, not caring to listen to the rest of Xavier's warning. I rushed past the people huddled in my sister's living room—most of them there to greet Sofia, I was sure—and finally reached Vivienne's bedside.

My senses went on overdrive the moment Sofia's eyes met mine. She was sitting on the edge of the bed, clutching Vivienne's hand as she fed Vivienne a vial of blood. For a moment, I couldn't return my focus back on Vivienne, because Sofia's presence was so overwhelming.

"Please leave…" I sounded like I was begging her. "I don't want to do something I'll regret."

Sofia nodded. I knew she understood why I needed to be away from her, but the truth gave little consolation. Still, she graciously obliged, helping my sister drink the last of the blood before sidestepping me and passing by to leave me with Vivienne.

I was using all my willpower just to stand still the moment Sofia passed me by. When the door shut behind her, I remained rooted to my spot for a few more seconds before I could gather my wits about me and make my way to my sister.

"Vivienne… I thought I'd lost you…" My voice broke as I held her hand.

She seemed frail and weak, a shadow of my vibrant sister, but she managed to smile at me as she squeezed my hand. "Derek… You look incredible."

"You're alive."

"I want to see Father, Derek. I have something important to tell him."

My gut clenched. How on earth was I going to tell her about everything that had been going on between our father and me? How was I to tell her that I'd taken over the kingdom, that I was now king of The Shade and Gregor was in a prison cell?

"Don't worry." Vivienne nodded. "I have a fair idea of what's happening. That's why I need to speak with him. It's a matter of great importance."

"I'll see it done," I promised.

"War is on the horizon, isn't it?" she asked, her blue-violet gaze settling on me with deep concern.

I nodded. "Yes. The other vampire covens are blaming me for what happened at The Oasis."

"Sofia told me about that. I'm disappointed that you left her with the hunters, Derek. With everything that's going on, the burden of finding true sanctuary falls on you. You're losing time. You can't afford to be apart from Sofia ever again. Sofia is your lifeline, Derek."

"I don't know how to be with her, Vivienne. I crave her so much. How can she remain by my side without me destroying her?"

"Haven't you learned your lesson yet? You are not strong enough to be away from Sofia. You can last for a time, but darkness will catch up with you, Derek. Make no mistake about it. Sofia is stronger than you give her credit for."

"It's not her weakness that I'm scared of. It's mine. How do I keep myself from devouring her?"

"Does she deny you her blood, Derek?"

I shook my head, remembering the last time she'd bared her neck to me, coaxing me to drink, allowing me to have my fill. "She willingly lets me have as much of her blood as I need."

"Then perhaps it would be better if you just partake of what she offers. Drink deep. Take what she gives."

"And what do I give her in return?" Every bit of me was against what Vivienne was saying. The thought of just going ahead and drinking as much of Sofia's blood as I craved made me sick. "I love her, Vivienne. How could I do that to her?"

"Maybe that love is enough for her, Derek." She smiled at me. "I'm tired. I'd like some rest now. Go to her. Stop tormenting yourself. Stop tormenting her."

She shut her eyes and I stood before leaning down to place a kiss on her temple. No words could express how grateful I was that she was there. I didn't even want to think about what she had been through—I was certain that I had plenty of time to be indignant. At that point, I was just thankful that I still had my twin, my ally—another Novak who wasn't out to torture me or dethrone me.

I stepped out of the room and all eyes found me. Gavin's, Ashley's, Sam's and Rosa's. Aiden's glare was fixed on me even as I shifted my eyes from him to his daughter. I didn't need to look at Sofia to know that she was there. I was aware of her presence, my heart pounding at the very scent of her.

I gulped as I looked into her emerald eyes. Vivienne's words echoed in my ear. *Drink deep.*

I lost control. Before I knew what was going on, I had her pinned to a wall, my hands on her hips, raising her up so that she was barely on her tiptoes, my fangs bared, ready to sink into the milky white skin of her neck.

I was about to take the bite I so longed for, but out of nowhere, I managed to scrounge up what was left of my self-control and step away from her. My thoughts cleared and I could hear her humming. She was humming our song—the same one I'd hummed to her the night of her eighteenth birthday—the night

I'd promised to find a way to be with her.

I stared into her lovely face, and realized once again how precious she was to me.

"You can control yourself, Derek," she whispered as she took my hand in hers.

My fangs retracted and jolts of pleasure shot through my spine when she reached up and gently pressed her lips against mine. She smiled at me before looking over my shoulder.

"I'm fine, Dad."

My heart sank. Aiden Claremont had just witnessed me attacking his daughter. I turned to find Aiden trying to get away from Sam and Ashley. Gavin, on the other hand, was holding a gun—one I was sure that Aiden had pointed at me when he saw me charge for Sofia.

Aiden was glaring daggers at me. "How many times have you done that to her? How many times have you pushed her against walls and sunk your fangs into her?"

I hung my head, recalling the numerous times I'd lost control with Sofia, the many times her life had been endangered.

To my relief, Sofia answered for me, "It doesn't matter, Dad. Derek and I are going to take a walk. You stay here. We're going to spend the night together. We need to catch up. I'll be fine."

"No." Aiden shook his head. "I'm not going to let you leave with that monster, not after what I just saw him do to you."

"This isn't hunter territory anymore. If Derek says he wants me with him, then there's really nothing you can do about it."

She squeezed my hand, but I was apprehensive.

"Maybe your father's right, Sofia... I don't know if I can control myself around you... I..."

She cupped my cheeks with both her hands and began shaking her head. "Derek... please..."

The thought that she wanted to be with me as much as I wanted to be with her was my undoing. How could I stand there and not give in to what she wanted? How could I ignore her plea?

I raised my eyes to Aiden's—his glare warned me to choose my words well, but Sofia was right. He was in my territory, where my word was law. I gave Sam and Ashley a quick look. "Kindly take Mr. Claremont to The Catacombs. I'm sure he'll be more comfortable in his daughter's quarters, where he'll be among humans, instead of here with the vampires. Rosa, make sure he is fed well. Gavin, kindly inform Xavier to keep an eye on Vivienne. Where's Claudia?"

"She returned to her villa," Sam responded. "We weren't quite sure what to do with her."

"She's no threat. She really just wants a way back into Yuri's good graces," Sofia explained.

"Leave her then. It's about time she realized how much Yuri values her." I looked at Aiden. "I will do your daughter no harm, sir."

He snorted. "Sure you won't."

I turned to Sam. "Sam, one more thing... See to it that my father is released and escorted to my sister's chambers. Make sure he is well-guarded by vampires stronger than him. We must also immediately hold a Council meeting to address the loss of our chilling chambers... We won't have enough blood to last us for another week unless we do something about that."

I didn't miss the way Aiden's eyes sparked with interest at that bit of information. I was sure every perceived vulnerability at The

Shade was a point of interest to a man like him.

Finally satisfied that I had all my bases covered, I walked out of the penthouse with Sofia. We were already in an isolated part of the woods when Sofia stopped in her tracks and looked up at me.

"You're trembling," she said in what was almost a whisper.

"It's nothing." I shook my head. "This cure... do you think it will work?"

"It worked with my mother. I saw it with my own eyes. She's not happy about it, but Ingrid Maslen is human again... She's still nothing like my mother was. She's one angry human..."

"How is that possible?"

"I don't know." She shrugged.

I wanted it to be true. I wanted to escape my immortality and the weight of being prophesied as some sort of savior to my kind. I was also aware that since Sofia could never be immortal, the only way we could be together was if I became mortal once again. My head was swimming with everything I wanted to say about Anna possibly being immune too, about Sofia not actually having LLI, but whenever I looked at Sofia, all I could think about was how much I wanted her blood.

"I can't stand this." She shook her head. "We can't keep being this guarded around each other."

I swallowed hard, wondering what it was that she had in mind. She stepped away from me and to my surprise, she began unbuttoning the top buttons of her red blouse. I knew what she was doing, what she was willing to let me do, and I began shaking my head.

"No... Sofia..."

She stepped forward and pushed me backwards until my back

hit a tree trunk. I couldn't remember her ever being so aggressive, but I didn't dare complain when her lips began to knead against mine—demanding and passionate, hungry for something that I myself was starving for.

I stopped fighting it and allowed my hands to fall to her waist. I pulled her up so that she didn't have to strain her neck just to kiss me. I responded with passion and hunger.

"You're mine, are you not?" she whispered breathlessly when our lips finally parted.

"You know I am," I responded, forgetting my craving for her blood as I tried to wrap my tingling senses around what had just happened.

"And I'm yours, am I not?"

I gulped before nodding. "I hope so..."

She pulled her blouse down her shoulder to expose her neck to me. "Then stop torturing both yourself and me, Derek. It's okay." She stepped forward and tilted her head to the side as she took hold of my hands and placed them on her waist. "Satisfy your craving."

I couldn't stop even if I wanted to. I took the bite, a mix of guilt and ecstasy coursing through me when she whimpered. When the blood flowed past my tongue and down my throat, it was pure bliss. Her blood was coursing inside me... restoring me, empowering me, completing me. She overloaded my senses when she once again began to hum our song to me. She ran her fingers through my hair, gently caressing it to assure me that she was all right.

Suddenly, I had the urge to look at her lovely face, so I pulled my mouth from her neck and took her wrist instead. I bit into it without bothering to ask her. She bit her lip against the pain and watched as I drank from her wrist.

Every sense I had was filled with Sofia Claremont—the scent of her, the feel, the taste, the sight, the sound of her sweet voice humming our song.

Eventually, I pulled my teeth out of her wrist and then grabbed her waist to pull her against me so I could kiss her again. It wasn't until our lips parted that the guilt began to sink in.

Sofia was the one who pulled away from the kiss. "Derek... are you crying?"

I tried to hold the tears back, but I couldn't. At the sight of the blood trickling from her neck and from her wrist, I broke down right in front of her. "How can we stay this way, Sofia?"

"The cure will work." She nodded, sounding like she was wishing it instead of actually believing it. "You won't have to do this anymore."

Suddenly, it felt like everything I had, everything I wanted, everything I could be, hung on this cure—a cure created by the hunters, whom I neither believed in nor trusted. A cure that I doubted could be possible.

Still, seeing the hopeful expression on my lovely girl's face, I couldn't help but adopt her hope. "I pray the cure works."

"It will, Derek. It will."

Neither of us missed the lack of conviction in her words. I wanted to believe in the cure as much as she seemed to, but I was afraid to hang my hopes on what could be just some ploy for the hunters to discover The Shade.

"I hope you're right, Sofia, because if you're not... I honestly think it will be the end of..." I hesitated, not wanting to hurt her any more than I already had.

"Of what, Derek?" She stepped backward, away from me, so that she could see the expression on my face. She was hurt and I knew it. "You? Us?"

"Everything."

CHAPTER 38: AIDEN

What the hell is wrong with you, Claremont? You just let your daughter run loose with the most powerful vampire alive—the vampire you know is craving her blood, the vampire you just saw attack her.

I glared at the guards standing by the doorway to the caves they'd brought me to—apparently my daughter's quarters.

It's not like I have any choice.

I leaned against the backrest of the recliner in her living room. Utensils clinked as the girl named Rosa kept herself busy preparing food in the kitchen. She was accompanied by Lily, a widow with two children—who all seemed to have lived at The Shade their whole lives. They'd already prepared a meal earlier that day, one I'd barely eaten due to my anxiety over what was happening to Sofia.

I kept pacing the floor, tormented by worst-case scenarios

regarding what the vampire could possibly be doing to my daughter. At some point, I took a nap, only to wake up and find the place still as dim as night, with Rosa and Lily cooking another meal—dinner, she said.

One of Lily's children approached me. She was introduced to me as Madeline, five years old. She had red hair that reminded me of Sofia's.

Madeline sat on the couch across from mine and stared at me. She was making me highly uncomfortable. "Does the sun ever rise here?" I asked her in a serious tone, hoping to scare her away.

She tilted her head to the side. "What's the sun?" she asked.

"You know… That big, shining light up in the sky…"

"You mean the moon?" She tilted her head to the side in thought. "Well, Mama rarely ever lets Rob and me out of The Catacombs, but when she does, I get to see the moon and the stars. I love it when the moon smiles." She gave me one big grin, showing me how she was missing one of her front teeth. "I've only seen the moon. No one ever told me about the sun—not even Gavin and he's out of The Catacombs a lot. The vampires like him."

"And they don't like you?" I raised a brow.

"Well, I don't know. Mama tells me to stay away from them. Ashley seems to like me though and so do Kyle and Sam, but Mama scolds me whenever I play with them. Gavin's my older brother and he gets to hang out with the vampires all the time—especially after he became friends with Sofia."

"Madeline, don't bother our visitor." Lily tried to pull the little girl away from me. She eyed me warily. "I'm so sorry, sir. She's normally not so comfortable around strangers, but she seems to like you."

"He's Sofia's father, Mama. And he's human... he won't bite me."

My heart went out to the five-year-old and the young mother trying to keep her in check. "How long have you been here, Lily?"

The dark-haired beauty bowed my way. "All my life, sir. I'm a Natural. We were born here. So were my parents and their parents before them."

"You have a lovely daughter."

"Aye. It's why I fear for her so much. Loveliness is a dangerous thing to have here, especially for a young girl."

My heart broke. I couldn't offer her salvation even if I wanted to. Slaves were considered dead to us. We annihilated them right along with the coven. If a hunter wanted to bother saving loved ones taken by vampires, they did it of their own accord, at their own risk.

"It's been a lot better since Sofia came. We never thought she would survive after being caught up in the rebellion, but she did." Lily smiled at me. "Your daughter saved a lot of lives. That day at the town square when Derek's father—he used to be our king..."

"Gregor Novak," I recalled.

Lily nodded. "Yes. Him. He wanted Sofia flogged—right along with my son and several of the other young Naturals who started the revolt. We all thought it would be the end of her. Her fragile body couldn't have taken all those blows. My heart leaped when Derek took the lashes for her. His back was unrecognizable after— you could barely tell which part was skin and which part bones... It was an awful sight, but we all knew then that he loved her and that as long as they were together, life here at The Shade would never be the same again. I never thought I'd hear myself saying that I love a vampire, but any vampire who is good in Sofia's book is good in mine."

"We like Sofia," Madeline piped up. "Even my brother, Rob, likes Sofia and he doesn't like many girls at all. He's seven. Andrea tried to kiss him and he was mighty angry."

I listened to the two talk on and on about my daughter and her heroic feats on the island. I wasn't sure I liked hearing how beloved Sofia was at The Shade. Their stories forced me to realize what I was taking from Sofia by forcing her away from the island and away from Derek.

I hated to admit it, but I saw then why she loved The Shade and its inhabitants so much.

Truth be told, I was impressed by The Shade. It didn't take a genius to see why it was so powerful. Unlike all the other covens, the island was self-sustaining. It had little contact with the outside world. It had a thriving human population seemingly loyal to the vampires—something my mind could not comprehend.

Of course, Lily made her fears clear. I knew she felt the same protectiveness for Madeline that I had for Sofia. At that moment, I found in her a kindred spirit fearful for her child as I was for mine.

"You need not fear, sir." Lily nodded. "Derek would never intentionally harm Sofia. He loses himself sometimes when he blacks out, but there's only one person who can reel him back to his senses, and that's your daughter. No one else is capable."

"King Derek needs Queen Sofia." Madeline had a sweet smile.

My stomach turned at the idea of my daughter having some sort of fairytale romance with the king of the vampires.

Right about then, Sofia and Derek stepped past the guards and into the room, their hands clasped, smiles on their faces.

The first thing I noticed was the bite marks on my daughter's neck. Despite whatever Lily and Madeline had told me about Derek, he still eradicated any hopes I had that their love could be real. I was livid at the thought of him once again feeding on my daughter.

"How dare you," I hissed as I began charging toward him. "You said you wouldn't harm her…" I caught a glimpse of her wrist and saw bite marks there too. I grabbed Sofia's wrist and raised it up to him. "Is this your idea of not harming my daughter?"

Derek was unable to look me in the eye. His display of shame only angered me further.

"Dad…" Sofia spoke before I could once again start a tirade. "It was my idea. I offered my neck to him. Don't take your anger out on him."

I stared at her with disbelief. "Sofia… I don't understand. How could you let him treat you this way?"

"If your cure works, then he won't have to drink from me ever again. It works, does it not?" she challenged me.

I gritted my teeth. "I need the hunters' scientists here. I cannot administer the cure on my own."

Sofia's face contorted with shock as she shook her head, letting go of Derek's hand and stepping forward. "You never said anything about needing them here. Why wouldn't you…"

"Would you have agreed to bring me here if I had said that I needed to bring a team of hunters with me? You saw that an entire team of people prepped Ingrid for the cure. I just gave her the final shot. I don't have enough expertise to do it myself. What if something goes wrong?"

This time, Derek stepped forward, standing right beside Sofia. He looked me straight in the eye and I couldn't help but shudder at the power and authority oozing from him. "How do we know this isn't all a trap?"

I shrugged. "If you're that desperate for the cure, then you'll just have to trust me."

Derek shifted his eyes from me to Sofia. "I don't trust him."

I was hoping that my daughter would take my side, but she eyed me warily. "Neither do I."

I was surprised by the effect her disapproval had on me. From Lily and Madeline's stories, I realized that Derek had proven that he was worthy of Sofia's trust. He had turned his back on his own father, saved her many times, risked his life to face Borys Maslen on his own turf just to rescue Sofia. She had reason to believe that he loved her.

What have I done for her other than order her around?

Sofia wasn't giving Derek her blind trust like I'd thought she was. He had done what he had to do to earn her loyalty.

I, on the other hand, had done nothing. My daughter had become a beautiful, strong young woman throughout her stay at The Shade. I certainly wasn't the person to thank for what she'd become.

But then, who was?

I eyed Derek from head to foot and grimaced. No matter what he had done for my daughter, I couldn't swallow down the thought of ever owing him anything.

If there's someone I need to thank for the beauty and strength of spirit I see in Sofia, it's certainly not him.

Chapter 39: Gregor

She's alive. My precious Vivienne is alive.

I couldn't believe my eyes. She was right there in front of me. My only daughter was alive. Seeing her smile—the same smile that had brought me through some of the darkest nights of the past five hundred years—made me break down in tears.

I'd never forgiven myself for what I had allowed myself to do to her so long ago, when I'd let Borys Maslen claim her as his betrothed. No other event in my life had made me feel weaker than when Borys had arrived to take her and I couldn't do anything but cower in his presence.

I should've fought for her. I should've done everything in my power to keep him from taking her, but I'd been unable. He'd taken her, he'd broken her, and if it weren't for Derek saving her, I probably never would've seen her again.

Derek had never forgiven me for it. I'd never forgiven myself for it, but Vivienne had. She was the one thing keeping our family together and when we'd thought her dead, we'd fallen apart. Lucas had lost his life at the struggle in The Oasis and Derek and I were very much willing to kill each other, but I'd spent the past centuries trying to make it up to my daughter, trying to be a good father, a good ruler, listening to her wise counsel.

I was lost without her and now she was back.

Vivienne's soft hands began brushing through my hair as I sobbed at the edge of the bed, kneeling on the floor beside her. She remained still until I could gather my composure and look at her.

"Vivienne... I never thought I'd see you again. What have they done to you?" I could barely speak the words out. I knew she was in pain and I hated not being able to do anything about it.

"I'm all right, Father." She struggled to sit up on the bed and I helped her, fluffing up the pillows behind her so she could sit comfortably.

No other person in the world melted my heart the way Vivienne did. I blinked away the tears as I sat next to her, putting my arm around her so that she could lean her head on my shoulder.

She snuggled against me and drew a deep breath. We sat silently for a couple of minutes. I reveled in once again holding her in my arms. With her, I felt accepted. While Derek and their mother had always made me feel like some sort of disappointment, Vivienne never had. I was her father and she loved me.

"I didn't think it was true." I placed a kiss on her head. "I didn't think you could've survived, but you did."

"Barely..." She chuckled dryly. "If it weren't for Sofia, I never would've gotten out of the haze they put me in."

I tightened my jaw at how she attributed her survival to the redhead my son was so madly in love with, the same young woman I hated with every fiber of my being.

"The darkness is coming for her," was all I managed to say.

At that, Vivienne scoffed. "It's been after her since the day she was born, Father."

I didn't understand what she was trying to tell me. When it came to her, I rarely did. Talk of Sofia Claremont made me sick to my stomach. "Do you know what your brother did to me? He took over ruling The Shade. He overthrew me and put me in prison."

"I'm sure he had good reason, Father."

Her words were a blow to my gut. I had forgotten how fiercely loyal she was to her twin. I couldn't blame her. *Derek was the one who risked his life to save her from Borys, not me. He was her savior, while I cowered in fear.*

"Father, was the prophecy not clear to you? We are supposed to support Derek if our kind is to survive. The Shade and all of its people are his to save and rule, not yours."

In the deepest recesses of my heart, I knew that what my daughter was saying was the truth. Only Vivienne was able to access those parts of myself that I had had to turn off in order to survive the past centuries, but her words were difficult to swallow. "Was everything I did for The Shade all those years for nothing, Vivienne?"

"Everything we did was to prepare for Derek's awakening, so that he could fulfill the prophecy and bring our kind to true sanctuary. I thought that much was clear to you, Father."

My jaw tightened as a battle waged inside of me—a battle I was afraid I could never win.

Vivienne knelt on the bed—slowly and carefully—so that she could face me and look into my eyes. The moment her blue-violet gaze bore into mine, I knew that she knew what was behind the mask of confidence I was trying to keep up.

Her face fell and a tear ran down her cheek. "The darkness has gotten to you, hasn't it?" she asked, her voice about to break.

I nodded, confirming her worst fears. She'd spent hundreds of years trying to protect me from the darkness and to look her in the eye and tell her that she'd lost me was heartbreaking.

"I'm so sorry, Father. I didn't think... I had hoped..." She choked on her own words and tears began streaming down her face.

I pulled her into my arms and let her sob into my chest, not knowing what to say to console her.

"Have I failed you so badly, Vivienne?" I asked, my own voice choked with the tears I was trying to hold back.

She shook her head into my chest and kissed me on the cheek. "No, Father. It's not too late yet. You can fight this, but you have to listen to what I'm saying. You have to be a father to Derek. He is not your nemesis. You need to honor the prophecies. If you fail in this, Father, the darkness is going to use you to destroy us all."

Her words made me sink into despair. Despite my fears, I nodded. She didn't have to know how weak her father was. She didn't have to know that it might be too late, that the darkness already had too firm a grip on me.

"I'll do that, Vivienne," I lied. "I can't allow myself to be your downfall."

Even as I said the words, a hiss echoed from within me—full of spite and with a hint of amusement.

You're a fool, Gregor Novak. Your weakness will destroy them all, and your beloved princess will be the first to fall.

Chapter 40: Claudia

I couldn't stand being inside my penthouse. It reminded me of how much I'd allowed darkness to take over me since I had turned into a vampire. I had become the monster I'd hated. I'd become the Duke.

The memories of everything that had happened here haunted me. All the horrors I'd put Ben, and so many young men like him, through began to replay in my mind. I could almost feel their presence inside my home.

I'd hated Lucas, but I'd reminded myself that I was just like him—evil to the core—so he was one of the few people who had frequented my home. Lucas had met a grisly demise back at The Oasis. The only other person was Yuri.

Thus, when I heard a knock at the door, I found myself shaking as I made my way to the door. I opened it and gulped when I saw Yuri standing on my doorstep.

I was expecting him to say something mean or give me a glare. We were known around The Shade for our frequent fights. This time, however, he just stared at me and I stared back.

When a tear ran down his cheek, it was my undoing.

"Yuri..." I choked out.

"I can't believe you left, Claudia."

I began to sob, because for the first time in the centuries I'd known Yuri, I felt completely vulnerable and exposed to him. I guessed I had always been. I'd just had trouble admitting to myself that he knew me more than I knew myself. He saw right through the hard exterior I'd been putting up.

"I'm so sorry, Yuri," I managed to say in between my sobs. "I never should've left. I was a fool. I just..." I wiped away my tears and tried to get a hold of myself. "I know how loyal you are to Derek. I should be too. After everything he's done for us... for The Shade... but I just..."

"Shut up, Claudia." He stepped into my home and closed the door behind him. "Just shut up. Stop torturing yourself over the past. You're back. That's what matters."

To my surprise, he grabbed me by the waist and lifted me into his arms and kissed me. Passionate at first, but he must have remembered who I was, because his kiss became gentle, tender... much like a sweet caress as his tongue pushed past my lips.

When our lips parted, I could feel myself blushing. He set me back down on the ground and both of us were in a stunned silence for a couple of minutes.

"Have you forgiven me, Claudia?"

"What do you mean?"

"For that night... That night when I..." He choked.

He didn't have to finish. I remained silent as I searched myself for an answer. "I couldn't forgive you until I realized how much I've made both you and myself suffer for my bitterness. I forgave you the moment I realized that you are the only man I've ever loved, Yuri, but I also know that I could never be worthy of you."

His face took on a grim expression as he shook his head. "Don't say that. You are the only woman I've ever wanted, Claudia."

He retrieved something from his pocket and my breath. The folded piece of parchment had become tattered and browned throughout the years, but it was still the symbol of a walk in the woods, an innocence stolen from both of us.

"This time, I won't take it back," he said, as he handed it to me.

Trembling, I took the paper and opened it up. Upon seeing it, I couldn't bear looking into his face. "How could you still want me, Yuri? I'm so broken."

"We're all broken, Claudia, but none of us are beyond fixing."

His lips once again pressed against mine and he whispered the words I'd longed to hear for centuries.

"Let me love you."

Chapter 41: Sofia

Dinner with Aiden was awkward to say the least. He was sitting at the head of the table and there seemed to be many things he wasn't comfortable about: Derek and I sitting next to each other and ignoring our food as we acted like the teenagers that we were—or at least I was—fooling around and playing footsie, or Rob making a face at us, or Madeline giggling with delight at how sweet we were.

Lily seemed pleased with us. Gavin didn't seem to care. Rosa was too busy staring at Gavin to notice. Ian and Anna decided to opt out of the awkwardness and eat elsewhere.

Aiden, on the other hand, expressed his irritation by banging his spoon and fork over his plate every chance he got.

"Are you drumming?" Rob asked. "Ian sometimes makes some music with a bunch of old cans. He's really good at it."

Aiden dropped his utensils on his plate, which he pushed

away so that he could lean his elbows on the wooden table. "So," he said. "You haven't told me whether you're going to let the hunters come…"

Derek and I exchanged uncomfortable glances.

"Well, we haven't discussed it properly yet. If you want an answer now, I think the answer is no." I shifted on my seat, gearing myself up for a confrontation.

"The sooner the hunters come, the sooner I get to administer the cure, the sooner we get out of here."

I raised a brow at my father. "We?"

"You're not saying that you're not coming back with me? I thought…"

"Dad… what would I do back at headquarters? Train to be a hunter? My life is here at The Shade."

"Sofia, you can't seriously be… You don't even have to stay at headquarters. I want you to live your life and it's not here."

"If the cure works, then Derek would be human too." I glanced at Derek and smiled, hope surging within me at the possibility of us being together. "If he decides to leave The Shade, then I'm going with him. If he decides to stay, then that's where I'll be."

I knew that I was tearing my father apart. I felt bad for him. He was my father and I loved him, but as much as I wanted to be a part of his life, I couldn't leave behind my own life to cater toward his hatred for the vampires.

"I'm sorry, but a life as a hunter isn't for me. Ben found that hard to accept too, but it holds true."

Derek took my hand underneath the table and squeezed hard. Aiden's shoulders sagged with disappointment. I guessed he knew me well enough to know that once I set my heart on something, there was no way he could dissuade me.

"Sofia and I will discuss the hunters' arrival tonight and let you know by breakfast, Aiden." Derek spoke up in an attempt to appease my father.

Aiden shot a glare at him. "You're not suggesting that my daughter will spend the night with you, are you?"

"Well..." Derek swallowed hard.

"What, so you can feed on her all night?" Aiden's eyes widened with horror. "You two haven't already slept together, have you?"

I coughed out the orange juice that I'd been drinking. I stood up. "I think that's enough dinner talk." Rob and Madeline were squealing with delight.

"I think we better go," Derek suggested and I quickly agreed.

We didn't wait for Aiden to object. Derek simply took my hand and whisked both of us out of The Catacombs and into the woods, where we took a long, leisurely walk back to his penthouse, where we planned to spend the night.

"Your father must be throwing a fit right now. I almost feel sorry for Rosa, Gavin, Lily and the kids," Derek said.

"They'll be fine." We walked in silence for a while, losing ourselves in our own thoughts, enjoying each other's company.

"Thank you for bringing Vivienne back." Derek broke the silence. "Claudia too. I'm not a big fan, but somehow The Shade isn't quite the same without her."

Derek and Claudia had always been at odds with each other. I knew that they'd slept together, but I doubted they even liked each other. Still, I understood what Derek was getting at. The

Shade had grown to be more than just a community. Over time, it had grown to be a family. They might not get along well with one another and everyone was always at each other's throats, but should anybody take one person away from the island, that person's presence—no matter how unpleasant—was bound to be missed. The familiarity with one another and acceptance of each other's flaws was what made The Shade feel like the home that it was.

Now, The Shade's falling apart. My heart sank at the thought. War was brewing, the blood supply was running low... The island wasn't going to be in its self-sufficient cocoon for long.

"What are you planning to do, Derek?" I asked.

He eyed me. "About what?"

I shrugged. "The Shade, the war, the blood supply... my father's proposal... the cure..."

He didn't reply immediately, and for a while, I thought he had no intention of replying at all. We just walked, listening to twigs snapping and leaves rustling beneath our feet.

"I don't know what to do," he finally admitted. "I solve one issue and another one pops up in its place. The last time something like this happened—right before I asked Cora to put the sleeping spell on me—I just gave in to the darkness so that I could control everyone through fear. I don't want to go back there."

I remembered what he'd shown me in his journals back at the Lighthouse—the history of The Shade, what had become of him, how he'd gone over to the dark side. I swallowed hard. I knew how important it was that he never go back to that version of him again.

"This cure, Sofia… Do you really think it's worth the risk of letting your father bring in more hunters to The Shade?"

My throat felt dry as I rasped my response out. "I want this to work out, Derek. Perhaps I'm being selfish with you… I don't know. It seems like the only way we can be together. I want to trust Aiden, but I'd be lying if I didn't admit that I don't. I'm scared that it's a trap."

"I can't even wrap my mind around the idea of a cure, Sofia. It feels like too big a risk. The other vampire covens have made it clear that they are uniting and gearing up for an attack. I don't know when, I don't know how, but they're coming and we need to be ready for that. The island is falling apart and we're barely keeping things together. If I allow hunters into The Shade and your father somehow betrays us… Do you realize what could happen?"

I nodded as I weighed his words. The atmosphere was charged with emotion. I could practically feel Derek's desperation oozing through me. I wondered once again if the cure really did work. *What if it works only with Ingrid?* I felt like I'd been played by Aiden, manipulated into trusting him and bringing him to the island—a place he'd been desperate to find since he heard about its existence.

"Even if the cure works," Derek continued, "what's going to happen? How am I going to defend the island as a mortal?"

I swallowed hard. I hadn't thought that far. Was I expecting that all the vampires would simply agree to turn back into humans? Was I expecting that Derek and I would just skip out of The Shade and live normal, human lives? If Derek turned back to a mortal, he'd be powerless to fight against all these forces coming at him.

I couldn't find answers to the concerns Derek was placing before me, and yet every bit of me screamed that this was the way, that this was as close as we could get to true sanctuary at the moment.

"You're supposed to take your kind to true sanctuary, Derek. That much we know is true, but what *is* true sanctuary?"

"You tell me." He shrugged a shoulder. "I don't really know anymore, to be honest. I used to think The Shade was true sanctuary."

"It can't possibly be true sanctuary. The last time I talked to Corrine, she told me that she was the last of the witches capable of keeping The Shade hidden. The island is safe from human detection and sunlight only as long as she is alive. The Shade's fall is inevitable."

Derek's bright blue eyes, illuminated by moonlight, focused on me, searching me for an answer. "I don't know what to tell you, Sofia." His shoulders sagged. "Perhaps this is it. Maybe true sanctuary is just an eternity of war and bloodshed, and once The Shade falls, I'm doomed to find one temporary haven after another to keep my subjects protected. Perhaps that's my fate. Forever."

I shook my head and stopped in my tracks to look him in the eye. "Derek, you can't possibly believe that's true."

"Maybe you're right... Maybe I need the cure... Maybe the only escape from this is mortality."

His words lit a fire in me that I couldn't extinguish no matter how hard I tried. I didn't know how to explain it to him or how to make sense of what was going through my mind, but I knew without a doubt that what he had just said was true. Mortality was Derek's true sanctuary.

Chapter 42: Ingrid

Bloody fools. They underestimated me.

I couldn't keep the smirk off of my face as I made my way through the secret passages that Aiden had introduced to me during our short love affair. Aiden's young protégé, Zinnia, had messed up big time when she had left me momentarily unguarded as I'd headed off to the showers. I knew how to find my way around the headquarters and quickly found my escape, emerging outside the gardens.

The moment I did, however, I had a big problem. It was the height of noon and the sun was blazing down on me. The moment its painful rays hit my skin, my suspicions once again proved true. I didn't know how it had happened, but Aiden's cure had failed. When I'd cut that glass into my skin and it had healed, I'd known that I was immortal, but when the sun began to irritate my pale skin, I knew that I was still a vampire.

I had to find a way out of hunter territory and out of the sun as quickly as possible. The sun's rays weakened a vampire immensely. It would take ten minutes before it would begin to get beneath my skin and the pain would be agonizing. It would be a slow, painful death.

Trying to ignore the sting of the sun, I used my agility as a vampire and scaled the nearby wall. I knew the hunters were already after me. I didn't have much time to get away. I jumped from the top of the wall to the ground below and ran with lightning speed. I ran, ignoring the pain of my skin peeling away. I ran even when I felt blood coming out of the sockets of my eyes. I ran until I could no longer run, until the sun had completely worn me down. It felt like hours until I collapsed on the ground, every bit of my body writhing in pain. I was miles away from hunter territory now, in the middle of a meadow, not certain where I was or how I was going to get out of there.

A log cabin stood on the horizon. The small house was only a couple of hundred meters away, but it felt like it was an ocean away. I dragged myself toward the home, my charred skin beginning to smoke, the pain of the sun digging in to my very bones. It felt like a million needles being repeatedly jabbed right through my skin to the core of my bones.

It took all of my might to drag myself toward the cabin. I wondered if it was a trap set by the hunters. I even thought that it could be some sort of optical illusion, but at that moment, whatever it was, that cabin was my only escape from the punishing rays of the sun.

I couldn't have imagined how grotesque I looked as I crawled up the front porch. It felt like all the liquids had been drained from my body and I was dried and shriveled up. One look at my hands made my stomach turn. Both looked like rotting flesh.

I pushed the door open and lost all control when a young woman who couldn't have been any older than Sofia descended a wooden staircase. She shrieked before I charged for her and devoured her, drinking down every single drop of her blood.

By the time I snapped out of my blackout, I was surrounded by three dead bodies and the sun was no longer shining. I couldn't help but smile as I rose to my feet. *I did it. I escaped hunter territory.* I sought out a mirror and was pleased to find my body restored, even though my skin was still stinging.

Gathering my wits about me, I knew that I had been lucky and that the hunters were surely still after me. I found a cell phone in the pocket of one of the teenagers I had killed. I searched the cabin for clues about its address before dialing Natalie Borgia's number.

My message to her was simple: "Wherever Borys is, let him know that I'm alive and that I need him to get me."

Within hours, a helicopter arrived. At first, I thought that it was the hunters' and I panicked, but when I saw Borys, I sighed with relief. I ran into his arms, tears streaming down my face.

He embraced me and pulled me against his chest as he whispered into my ear, "I thought I'd lost you, Ingrid."

I once again felt the strength and security that I could only feel when I was around the vampire who had sired me. I sobbed into his shoulder for a few seconds before whispering into his ear, "I think I know how you can get your hands on Sofia. Do you still want her?"

I could hear the spite and menace in his voice when he

responded in a low voice, "I've never wanted anything more than to feel her lovely, trembling form in my arms again."

I shuddered when I realized the hell Sofia was going to go through should Borys ever get a hold of her again. I swallowed hard as I remembered my daughter telling me she loved me. I dreaded the day that Borys would once again have Sofia within his grasp.

But it's too late, Ingrid. You have no choice but to surrender her to him.

Chapter 43: Gregor

The moment I was taken from my daughter's chambers and brought back to The Cells, I knew that I was in trouble. An odd mixture of determination to not disappoint Vivienne and pure terror began battling for the right to rule my will.

I shivered just thinking about what I had gone through between when I had left The Oasis and when I had finally returned to The Shade. If there ever was any doubt in my mind that we vampires were creatures of the dark, it had been totally eradicated when I was forced to come face to face with what a dark creature I had become. Darkness had taken hold of both Borys and me in a way I had never thought possible. It had taken full control.

Perhaps this is what happened to Derek before he decided to escape to his slumber. It's the reason he was so powerful. Darkness gripped him and made him the heartless leader who saved The Shade.

Clarity had come over me the moment I had looked upon Vivienne's blue-violet eyes. Her unconditional love for me as her father had awakened what little shred of humanity I still had left in me. The only reason I was thinking beyond the darkness' control was because Vivienne illuminated something deep within me. One small spark was all it took to light up pitch darkness.

However, my match was quickly running out of its flame. I was about to lose myself again. I would once again forget the love I felt for my children—especially Derek.

Alone in my cell, moonlight streaming from the small, barred window, I felt like a million voices were ringing in my ears all at the same time. I knew the kind of power I was up against. I knew the hold it had over me. This was a battle I couldn't win, but couldn't afford to lose either.

For the first time in the past five hundred years, I realized how I, as a creature of the dark, craved so much for light. I was desperate to keep the spark inside me burning.

Traitor, a voice whispered—coming from within me rather than from my surroundings. I shuddered. I tried to fight it. I tried to summon all the willpower I had within me to keep myself in control. I couldn't do it.

My body was no longer my own. Claws came out of my hand, and with my forefinger, I began scratching a message on my arm. My claw cut deep. I bit my lip against the pain as the message took form.

You chose the wrong side.

Chills ran down my spine as it dawned on me exactly what it meant. At that moment, I knew without a shadow of a doubt that there was no way I could make it through the night, and yet I felt an unnerving calm. I had been able to hold Vivienne in my arms again. I had been able to see her beautiful eyes and her calming smile.

Should I die that night, in the final moments of my life, I had chosen light.

CHAPTER 44: DEREK

As we lay in my bedroom, she was silent. She was soothing calm amidst a raging tempest. She peered at me through her long lashes and I found myself breathless.

Suddenly, the waves crashing over me seemed less threatening, the winds blowing at me seemed a little gentler. The storm surrounding me ceased to matter. Sofia was once again in my arms, serving as my calming center.

Her lips pressed against mine, and I knew that if I wanted to take it further she would happily give in, but I didn't want that. Not with her. I was determined to stay true to my vow that I would not make love to her until after she'd become my wife. It was my way of setting her apart from all those other women who came before her. It was my way of honoring her.

The idea that she could be my wife—in light of the hunters' newfound cure—thrilled me. To live a lifetime with Sofia, tasting her, loving her… It was far more than I could ever dream of, far greater than my deepest wishes even as a human. It had taken centuries to finally find her, but if that was all my immortality was good for, then it was worth it.

When our lips parted and she blushed the moment our eyes met, I could swear my heart stopped. I had no idea how I could've convinced myself that I could ever stand being apart from her.

"I was a fool to leave you," I admitted.

She nudged my shoulder. "Damn right you were. I was going crazy trying to understand why you left." Her voice broke. "You didn't even say goodbye."

"You wouldn't have let me go if I had."

"That's because we belong together, Derek. I can't believe you still don't know that."

"I couldn't stand the idea of preying on you, Sofia." My heart sank as I recalled my need to have a taste of her blood the moment I had woken up. I hadn't even asked her. I'd just taken what she was offering. "Does it hurt when I drink from you?" I asked, wondering why I even bothered. *Of course it hurts.*

"The bite stings at first, but it's not like I'm not used to it." She sat up on the bed and began pulling her hair up in a high ponytail.

I breathed out a sigh, hoping that we could freeze that moment and just stay cocooned in my bedroom, forget all the concerns that I needed to deal with. Of course, that was impossible. Right at that very moment, people shuffled outside my room, waiting for me to emerge. I guessed that it was some of the Elite—perhaps to discuss our severe lack of blood supplies. Just the thought of having to deal with all the drama made me groan out loud.

Sofia, who was already up and getting ready for the day, looked my way and chuckled. She leaned over my side of the bed and kissed my cheek. "We're together again, and that's all that matters right now."

She stepped into the bathroom and close the door behind her. I loved that about Sofia. She made the heaviest of situations feel lighter.

My ray of sunshine was back and I wanted to kick myself for allowing things to go any other way.

By the time we both got ready and stepped out of the bedroom, a group of people waited for us in the dining room—Cameron, Liana, Xavier, Eli, Yuri and to my surprise, Vivienne.

"Aren't you supposed to be resting? Sofia and I were just planning to visit you."

"Liana came over and told me about the island's blood supply. What are we going to do about that?"

I gave Liana a cold glare for worrying Vivienne. "That's what we're about to figure out today, Viv." I pulled out a chair for Sofia beside mine before taking a seat at the head of the table. "Before I ask to what I owe the pleasure of this invasion, do you have any suggestions regarding how we're going to fix this mess?"

I was greeted by a tense silence. There was a time when the answer would've been to abduct humans to feed on or to hold a culling—killing off all the weak and useless humans and draining them of blood that we could preserve at the chilling chambers. Now, none of us had any idea how to replenish the blood supply at such short notice. Until Sofia shrugged. "I don't see what the problem is."

All eyes turned to her.

Xavier seemed irritated. "Do you have any idea how thirsty I am, Sofia? I only had one packet of blood left and I had to give it to…" He bit his lip and caught his words as he glanced at Vivienne. "Not that I regret it, of course, but not all of us have a fresh supply of blood like Derek since you came back."

My gut clenched as I followed Xavier's eyes to the bite marks on Sofia's neck.

"What Xavier's trying to say is that if the vampires don't get their blood, we won't be able to keep them from attacking the humans at The Catacombs. We're going to have another riot, and considering that the hunters are coming and so are the other covens, we can't afford that," Liana summarized before taking in a deep breath.

"Yes. I get the dilemma," Sofia said. "I just don't know why you can't see the solution when it seems obvious."

"Just tell us what you have in mind, Sofia. We're all ears," I said.

"For one thing, you could always live on animal blood. Vivienne has survived all these years on that." Sofia raised her hands in the air before anyone could object. "Yes, yes. I know what you're going to say. Not everyone can do what Vivienne is doing. I get that. I do have another idea. I'd like to believe that through the past year, we've established some rapport between the humans and the vampires. I don't see why the humans wouldn't agree to donate their own blood to feed the vampires."

"You mean humans voluntarily letting vampires suck their blood?" Yuri scoffed.

"I think Sofia is saying that we replenish the stocks by getting blood from the humans the way hospitals and blood banks do." Eli glared at Yuri.

"Do you really think the humans would agree to that?" I asked Sofia.

"I don't see why not."

"One problem there." Vivienne sat up. "The vampires will end up craving whoever donated blood to them."

Sofia shrugged. "Well, it's a temporary measure, is it not? If the cure works, then it wouldn't be a problem."

"Ah, yes… The cure…" Liana nodded. "That's why we came here. So much hangs on whether this cure works."

"Well, if this cure is for real"—Cameron straightened up on his seat—"then Sofia's right. We wouldn't have to worry about blood supplies at all."

"More than that," Liana added, "we won't need the protection of The Shade anymore. The other covens can attack all they want… It won't matter. They can even turn back into mortals if they please."

"The hunters won't have to hunt us down anymore." Yuri leaned back in his seat, arms crossed over his chest, his brows furrowing in deep thought.

"A cure just might end all of this," Liana concluded.

Finally, Cameron got straight to the point. "I guess what we're trying to say is that we think we ought to look into the possibility of this cure being real, because it is far better than a full-on war with both vampire covens and hunters."

My jaw tightened. They were listing all the advantages of the cure being real, advantages I'd been mulling over since I had heard of the cure. Sofia and I exchanged glances and I could tell that she was feeling the pressure.

"So I guess we're going to let more hunters into the island?

We're going to risk that?" I directed my attention toward Vivienne. "What do you think, Vivienne?"

My sister shook her head. "I don't know. I'd be lying if I said that I trust the hunters, because I don't."

"I don't trust them either," Sofia said. "But…"

"… the cure may be our last hope," Eli finished for Sofia. "A war would end us."

"How are they even going to do it?" I couldn't help but blurt out. "I can't even wrap my mind around how the other covens plan to attack us without being detected by humans. A war would *definitely* attract attention."

Eli lifted his glasses over the bridge of his nose as he shifted in his chair, rubbing his neck. "I can't be sure, but…" He hesitated.

I narrowed my eyes at him. "But what, Eli?"

"I don't know… It's just… I don't think we're up against just the covens."

At this, Xavier, who seemed unable to pry his eyes off of Vivienne, snapped to attention. "What are you saying?"

"The other covens wouldn't dare risk something as big as this. That's what kept us safe from them all these years. You forget that a lot of vampires who migrated to The Shade from other covens warned us that the other covens coveted what we have here. A full-scale war isn't something anybody would risk unless…"

"… unless there's a greater influence backing them up." Vivienne nodded.

"Exactly," Eli said.

I froze. "You can't possibly mean…"

Eli and Vivienne exchanged glances.

Vivienne sealed my fears. "Great darkness is behind this."

I swallowed hard, realizing that I was up against a power far above what I could handle. I knew whom they were referring to, but it seemed impossible—surreal.

"I don't understand," Sofia said.

"They're referring to the original."

"The original?"

"The very first vampire."

CHAPTER 45: SOFIA

As soon as the words came out of Derek's mouth, someone began pounding at the front door. Derek and I stood in unison, worry creasing our faces.

When the door swung open, we found Sam looking breathless. "You're going to want to see this. At the town square."

"What's going on?" Derek asked.

"It's your father."

Derek shot a look at Vivienne. "Stay here, Vivienne." He cast a glare at Xavier. "Keep an eye on her."

Xavier nodded, looking as if he would rather die than let Vivienne out of his sight. Derek took my hand and pulled my body against him in a tight embrace so he could speed from the Pavilion to the Vale where the town square was.

The moment we arrived, I wished he hadn't brought me with him. It took every ounce of my willpower to keep myself from vomiting at the grotesque sight in front of me. Right in the middle of the town square was Gregor Novak's corpse, impaled on a stick. His heart, still beating, was right at the tip of the stick.

I could barely stand on my own feet, so when Derek's knees buckled, we both sank to the ground.

"Who would do this?" I muttered under my breath. That was when I noticed that something was scrawled on his arm, which looked like it was already rotting.

Derek, who didn't seem to have the stomach to approach his father's lifeless form, turned toward Sam. "What's written on his arm?"

Sam hesitated before responding. "It says, 'You chose the wrong side.'"

I couldn't understand what that meant. Whichever side Gregor was on, it certainly wasn't Derek's. Had Gregor somehow crossed someone else other than Derek? Derek couldn't have had anything to do with this grotesque crime.

Corrine emerged among the gathering crowd in the town square. Her brown eyes locked with Derek's, a grim expression marring her lovely face. From the very moment I'd first met Corrine, nothing seemed to shake her. Now her olive skin paled and for the first time since I had met her, I was certain that we were up against a force that was more powerful than her.

Chills ran down my spine and dread unlike anything I'd ever felt before swept over me. I stared up at Derek, knowing deep inside that both of us would break before we could be made whole again.

Alarm was in Derek's eyes when he broke his gaze with Corrine in order to look at me. "Sofia, you're trembling."

I hadn't been aware of how tightly I was squeezing his arm. I shook my head, not knowing how to articulate to him what was going through my mind. Even if I could, I didn't know if it would be wise.

I once again caught sight of Gregor's body, which was now being pulled from the pole it was impaled on. Despite all my apprehensions, I nodded resolutely. I needed to have faith. I couldn't afford not to have it. "We're going to make it, Derek."

When he pulled me closer to him and pressed his lips against my temple, I took it as reassurance that I was right.

The rest of the morning wore on with Eli and Liana working with Gavin and Ian, trying to figure out how to make the blood drive happen. Xavier, Cameron and Derek saw to arrangements about Gregor's body. Last time I'd caught a glimpse of Yuri, he was taking a walk with Claudia—something that I found delight in. On the other hand, I was left to deal with my father and all the questions he had about what had gone on between Derek and me last night.

"You let him drink your blood again, didn't you?" was the first thing Aiden asked me the moment I settled myself in the dining room of my chambers at The Catacombs.

Well, I didn't exactly let him. I woke up to find that he was already having his fill. Of course, I wasn't about to tell Aiden that. "Do we have to go through this again?"

Aiden's lips shut tight and we ate breakfast in silence without a word being exchanged until he finally asked the question that had probably been burning through his thoughts all night. "Is he allowing the hunters to come?"

"Do you have any idea at all how much is hanging in the

balance should this cure be for real?"

"You saw Ingrid turn back into a human, Sofia. With your own eyes! I don't understand how you could still hold so much doubt after witnessing something like that."

"What if it only works on her? What if it doesn't work on all vampires?"

"We won't know until we try, will we?"

I couldn't fight back the uneasy feeling I had over the whole matter. I wanted to believe Aiden, but this dread inside kept nagging at me. "I hope you understand that Derek means everything to me. You betray him, you betray me."

"I know that, Sofia. I also hope that you realize that you are my daughter and I will always fight for what I believe is best for you." He paused for a moment before continuing. "I know I messed up big time. I know I wasn't a good father to you, but I want that to change. I want you to trust me."

I couldn't bear shooting him down after what felt like one of the most sincere things he'd ever told me. Hesitantly, I nodded and gave him the signal to go ahead with something that could end us all.

"Have the hunters come."

CHAPTER 46: DEREK

I dragged myself through the entire day. The heavy weight that had settled on my chest the moment I'd realized that I had just lost my father was inescapable. I'd always been at odds with Gregor Novak, but I had never wished such a death on him. I had no idea how to face Vivienne. I wasn't even sure if she'd already been told. I sure didn't want to be the one to break the news to her. The mere thought of seeing her tears over the passing away of our father was more than I knew how to handle.

It seemed that it was the hand I'd been dealt. *Fix one problem and another will pop up. You're not even allowed time to just gather yourself together and pick the pieces up before the next tragedy.*

By the end of the day, I was ready to escape into sleep—the only recourse that would allow me to shut all my anxieties, fears and doubts out. I momentarily entertained the idea of going to Sofia at The Catacombs, but sleep seemed to be a more enticing escape than even my lovely redhead, who for certain was with Aiden, someone who would once again remind me about what I was already deeply guilty about. I could still feel Sofia's blood coursing through me. I was certain that it was the wellspring I was drawing life from throughout that day. It was also my deepest source of shame.

I just want to escape. From all of it. For a few hours, I want to be rid of all of this.

Xavier had gone with me to the Pavilion—most likely to check on Vivienne, who was being looked after by Liana. When he realized that I was off to my own penthouse, Xavier called me out on it. "Aren't you even going to check on Vivienne?"

I tensed at the thought. "I don't know if I can..."

"You have to, Derek. If there's anyone who can understand what you're going through, it's her. And it's your comfort and presence that she needs most right now. She'd only just wrapped her head around Lucas' death at The Oasis. She needs you."

I knew he was right, so despite the ache I felt inside, I obliged. I made my way to my sister's penthouse and found her inside her greenhouse, amidst her beloved orchids, roses, lilies and tulips. Her blue-violet gaze was misty with tears.

"Vivienne..."

She looked up and the moment she laid eyes on me, she broke down crying. She approached me and threw her arms around my neck. I wrapped my hands around her waist and pulled her against me, allowing her to sob as long and as much as she needed to. I found myself hoping that my presence was enough, because I couldn't find the right words to comfort her.

"It's just you and me now," she rasped out in between sobs.

"We're the last of the Novaks."

I hung my head—as if it was my fault Gregor was gone.

When her sobs subsided, she pulled away from me, her eyes fixed on a black orchid which she was caressing with her thumb. "I knew it would happen," she said. "He was too far into the dark. He was fighting with every bit of his strength to stay in the light, but even you weren't strong enough to stand against it when it began to consume you. He'd been giving into it for too long."

"I don't understand…"

Vivienne caught my eye in that way only she could—that way that made me feel as if she were looking into the depths of my soul. I would look into her eyes and find uncharted galaxies behind them. I could never really grasp her depth.

"I think he chose us, Derek. That's why he's dead. That explains the message on his arm. He chose us over darkness."

"He hated me," was all I could manage to say as I fought back my own tears.

Vivienne shook her head. "He lost a lot of himself. I know he wasn't the greatest father, but he did the best he could. He was a weak man. He was nothing like you, Derek. He never hated you. He envied you."

I smiled bitterly. "It doesn't matter now, I guess…"

She heaved a sigh and brushed her hand over my face. "I guess what matters is that we still have each other. No matter where our father is right now, I'm certain that he is much more free than he ever was as ruler of The Shade and father of the great Derek Novak."

Overcome by emotion, I could no longer keep the tears back. I pulled Vivienne against me. "I'm so glad you're back, Vivienne. I would have no idea how to get through this without you."

"You'll do just fine, Derek. You've always been stronger than any of us. Now that you have Sofia back here, you can make it. You can go against the original."

I pulled away from our embrace, my jaw dropping involuntarily. "You can't mean that... Vivienne..."

She just smiled at me and turned away. She'd said her piece and that was it. I was dismissed.

Going against the original vampire had never crossed my mind. I couldn't understand why she would even think it. The original was almost a myth to us. None of us knew if the creature really existed or what it was capable of. It was one thing to battle against something tangible, it was a whole other thing to contend with a powerful unknown.

I was in a daze as I returned to my penthouse, sleep leaving me. I couldn't escape to slumber even if I wanted to. Vivienne had just dropped a bomb that would make me toss and turn all night.

Thus, I was relieved to open my bedroom door and find Sofia sitting on the bed. My guitar was laid on the empty space on the bed beside her. She was busy penciling a drawing on the sketch pad laid over her lap, loose strands of her red hair falling over her face. She looked up through her long lashes the moment I entered and smiled.

"Rough day, huh?"

"As rough as it gets." I leaned against the doorpost. "I haven't been able to rise up from one wave crashing over me before another one comes raging toward me."

She tapped on the guitar beside her. "It's been a while since I last heard you play."

No matter how exhausted I felt, I wanted nothing more than to surround myself with that which I loved—music and Sofia. I sat on the edge of the bed and took the guitar. I began strumming a chord to make sure it was in tune. Satisfied that it was, I began to pluck, losing myself in the sound of the music.

Sofia settled behind me, leaning her chin on my shoulder as she watched me play. As I continued to play tune after tune after tune, she began whispering encouragements in my ear. "You're strong. Brave. Courageous. You don't need to give in to the darkness in order to get through this. I know you. We can make it through this. We're going to fight this together."

I had no idea how long it took before we eventually settled down on the bed, snuggling against each other, enjoying that reprieve. We were each other's refuge and in that bedroom, holding Sofia in my arms, it felt as if the world was as it should be.

"The hunters are coming tomorrow," Sofia whispered as she brushed her fingers over my chest. "You ready for that?"

"I don't know… Are you? If things go south, Sofia, I may need to fight your father… I just…"

"It's fine," she cut me off. "I know you have to do what you have to do."

I knew it was tearing her up to even think of having to choose between me and her father. "You don't have to choose, you know. I understand."

"I know, but you know that I'd choose you in a heartbeat, don't you?"

Her loyalty and love for me astonished me. And it meant the world to me to hear her say it. I placed a kiss on her forehead. "I love you so much, Sofia."

She smiled up at me. "I know… I want you to start believing that I love you just as much, Derek."

Her words were like a punch in the gut as I realized that by leaving her back at hunter territory, I'd showed her that I didn't believe in her love for me. I'd made the choice without her, leaving her out of the equation. I'd been unfair to her and I decided right then that it would never happen again.

We had a rough ride ahead of us, but somehow, that night, I realized that I didn't need to worry about tomorrow. I was fine where I was, because no matter what threats were coming our way, I had Sofia in my arms. Just like Sofia, I needed to live in the moment and love every minute of it.

I wished I'd known that earlier, before I'd wasted my immortality, but I guessed there was no better time to start than now.

Chapter 47: Sofia

We were at the Port. All of the Elite Council was present to defend Derek should there be a fight. The cure was going to be tested at the Port so that the hunters wouldn't have access to the island the way Aiden did.

The moment the group of six hunters emerged from the submarine, they revealed their faces, except for two, who remained hidden under hooded cloaks. The secrecy made me queasy. From the way Derek was staring at the two hooded hunters, he too sensed something was amiss.

Our suspicions were confirmed when Aiden, who was standing beside me, shouted out, "I don't know these people. These aren't hunters."

No sooner had the words come out of his lips when one of the "hunters" lunged for me. Before I could make sense of what was happening, an arm choked my neck, a familiar voice speaking out.

"We came here for her and her alone. You either give us a way out of here or she dies."

The chill of his breath and the depth of his gravelly voice made it clear who was holding me hostage. *Borys Maslen.*

My gaze instinctively locked with Derek's and I found in the blue depths of his eyes a mixture of fury and terror. Panic overwhelmed me at the idea of once again being taken captive by Borys Maslen. His mere touch was causing goosebumps to form all over my body.

"How…" Derek gasped out, perhaps wondering how on earth vampires—Borys Maslen at that—were even able to get into the submarines without getting recognized.

"Surprised, Novak?" Borys grinned, his breath cold against the back of my ear. "Since you helped the hunters destroy The Oasis, we've been getting some outside support. A beautiful witch's spell kept us disguised as hunters until we could reveal ourselves to you. Now let us leave with young Sofia here and no one has to get hurt. If you don't let us go, well, I'll just have to kill her."

He began nudging me toward the exit that would lead to the submarine, so I was relieved to find that the way to the submarines had been blocked by several of The Shade's guards.

"There's no way you're getting out of here with Sofia," Derek yelled.

From the look in his eyes, I had no doubt in my mind that I would see hearts ripped out.

"So you'd rather see her die than leave with me?" Borys traced a claw over my bare arm, causing blood to trickle. "And I thought you loved her."

"What do you want from her?"

"I want what is mine." He kissed me on the cheek and tears trickled down my cheeks as everyone around me watched helplessly. "But to be honest, I'm not the only one who wants her away from you, Novak. You're up against much more powerful forces now."

I swallowed hard at what he was implying. *The original.* The desperation in Derek's face was tearing me apart. I knew it was killing him to see me in Borys' grasp, even more now that the original was involved.

"She's my daughter." Aiden took a step forward. "Let her go. If she belongs with anyone, she belongs with me."

The other hooded "hunter" chuckled. I didn't need to know who it was. *Ingrid.*

"Did you really think your cure would work?" She grinned. "There's no cure, and lest you forget, she's my daughter too."

"This is getting exhausting." Borys once again clawed through my skin—so deeply, I couldn't keep in a scream. "Are you going to let us go or not?"

Despite the anguish in his eyes, Derek shook his head. "No."

"Can't you stop him?" Aiden hissed at Derek.

"It will take only a couple of seconds for me to break Sofia's neck," Borys explained matter-of-factly. "He can't risk that. I'm going to give you time to think this through, Novak. I'll give you an hour to let us all go unharmed." Borys began backing up to the cells at the Port, Ingrid and the other vampires with him. "Until you decide, my lovely Sofia and I are going to spend some private time together, heh? Think of all the fun we can have in a whole hour..."

Just like that, I found myself locked in a room with Borys, five vampires standing guard right outside the door.

"What do you want from me?" I spat at him after he pushed me to the ground.

"Many things, Sofia." He chuckled. "Many things. But first…" He licked his lips and bared his fangs. As if the implication wasn't already sickening, he pulled off his shirt and unbuttoned his jeans. I knew what he wanted, but I wasn't going to allow him to have it.

Gritting my teeth, I shook my head, determined to fight with every bit of my strength. *He's not going to make a victim out of me. Not again. Over my dead body.*

Chapter 48: Derek

I paced the Port's control room as I tried to figure out what to do. Just the thought of what Borys was doing to Sofia in that cell was enough to drive me mad.

"What are we going to do?" Aiden asked.

"Did you do this?" I didn't care that he was her father. If he had deliberately put Sofia in danger just to get to me, I'd break his neck.

He shook his head. "I don't understand what happened. They must have found a way to intercept my communication with the hunters. I had nothing to do with this."

I narrowed my eyes at him as I moved closer to him. "Is there really a cure, Aiden? Why is Ingrid a vampire again?" I was fighting the urge to choke him.

The man stood proud and indignant, unwilling to be intimidated even by me. He looked me straight in the eye.

"There's no cure, Derek. There can never be a cure to a curse such as yours."

I hit him across the face, making him fall on the ground— several feet away from me.

He coughed blood. "I just wanted what was best for Sofia. You're not what's best for her. I had to do everything I could to get this idea of a cure out of her head, to get you out of her system."

"You want what's best for her?" I pointed toward the room where she was trapped with Borys Maslen. "Do you have any idea what he could be doing to her right now? Do you have any idea how sick a monster Borys Maslen is?" I had no idea what to do. I could take down all of Borys' vampires if I wanted to, but Borys wouldn't hesitate to kill Sofia. I grabbed clumps of my own hair as I screamed out in frustration.

"We need to get her as far away from Borys as possible," I managed to mutter.

"Well, for once, we agree on something," Aiden said.

I wanted to strangle him."This is your fault. You know that, right?" I was about to march right toward him again, but a calm, female voice stopped me.

"Calm down, Derek. We won't get anywhere blaming each other."

I turned toward the voice and found Vivienne standing inside the room.

"What are you doing here? Vivienne, if Borys Maslen sees you…"

"I saw a vision of this happening. I rushed here, but I guess it's too late. He has her now."

"I don't know what to do, Vivienne. I want to kill something… anything…" Out of the corner of my eye, I could make out Aiden rising to his feet. *He would be a good first candidate.* "Just thinking of what he could be doing to her…"

A bang came from inside the cell and my heart plummeted, my fists clenching.

Ingrid came through the hallway and stepped into the control room. She eyed Aiden from head to foot, then smirked in triumph. "You didn't think you could keep me trapped in hunter territory forever, did you? After I escaped, I found a way to intercept your communication with Zinnia—she isn't exactly the brightest bulb, is she? Well, anyway… here we are. I won."

"What exactly did you win, Ingrid?" Aiden spat. "Does it really give you pleasure to see your own daughter being tormented by that monster?"

"You should see her put up a fight. She's in a pretty bad state."

Despite her words, I could swear that Ingrid hesitated, as if she was also being tormented by what Sofia was going through. She even seemed proud that Sofia was putting up a fight—something that made my heart leap and my gut clench at the same time.

Ingrid turned toward me. "Sofia is going to fight to her last breath before she allows Borys to lay a hand on her. I'm not sure she'll last an hour. Are you really sure you want to drag this out?"

"There's no way I'm going to let Borys leave this island with her."

"He will be more than willing to break every bone in her body and force her to drink his blood so she'll heal, then do it all over again. An hour is a long time, Derek." Her shoulders sagged and it was easy to see that she was conflicted. "Let us go."

I narrowed my eyes at Ingrid and wondered if she was really pleading for Sofia's sake. "I know Sofia. She would rather die than leave this island with Borys. I would rather die than give her over to him—not after what she has already gone through, not after you just told me what he's capable of doing to her." I couldn't help but look at her like she was stupid. "Are you even thinking straight? How could you leave your own daughter in the hands of the likes of him?"

"We're wasting time," Aiden interrupted, eyes brimming with tears. "We have to stop him from destroying Sofia." His voice was choked, and it was the first time I was convinced that he genuinely cared for Sofia.

"Let me talk with him." Vivienne took a step forward. "There was a time when it was me he wanted. Maybe we can talk him into taking me instead of her."

My eyes widened in horror. "Vivienne!"

"Can you think of any other way to get his eyes off Sofia even for a while? We have to at least try something…"

Another bang came from the room and I found myself fighting the urge to just barge my way into the room to kill Borys myself.

"You would do that for my daughter?" Aiden was looking at Vivienne as if she was some sort of miracle.

Ingrid, on the other hand, eyed her from head to foot. "What makes you think Borys would still want you when he has his immune right in his hands?"

"Borys wants Sofia because she's immune, right?" I took a step forward. "We have another immune on the island. If we bring her to him, would he consider her instead of Sofia?"

Ingrid seemed to take the proposal into consideration and

nodded. "I can ask him. Still... he's going to put Sofia through hell until this 'other immune' comes..."

Vivienne once again asserted herself—much to my chagrin. "Let me go with you... I can at least divert his attention from her for a little while."

Ingrid smirked at my sister, but shrugged. "If you really want to. I don't think you'll be of much help though... He'll probably kick you out of the room as soon as you show your face."

I couldn't understand why Vivienne was putting herself at risk on Sofia's behalf once again, but I was out of ideas and I was desperate to get Sofia out of the pain she was going through. "Vivienne, what are you even planning to do? You're nowhere near as strong as Borys."

"The point is to get his attention away from Sofia. The fact that I'm no threat to him is to my advantage."

I admired her courage, and yet the idea of sending my sister off to what could be her death didn't sit well with me. *I just got her back and now I have to send her to this monster.*

I glared once again at Ingrid. "She's your daughter. How could you..."

She rolled her eyes. "Please. Don't remind me. If you're trying to appeal to my maternal instincts, trust me... it won't work."

Aiden attested to this. "She isn't Sofia's mother. Camilla is dead."

I had to make a decision quick, because just as the words came out of Aiden's mouth, Sofia gave a piercing scream.

A sweeping cold ran up from the base of my spine to the back of my head. I pointed at Vivienne and blurted out, "Go! Now!"

I didn't care what had to be done that day. I wasn't about to lose Sofia.

No matter what, Borys Maslen wasn't going to leave The Shade alive.

I am going to rip him to shreds.

And I was going to relish every moment.

Chapter 49: Sofia

He's going to kill me.

When the back of his hand hit my face, I was surprised that my neck didn't snap. My head spun from the pain that racked my body. I had at least one broken rib and the parts of my body he dug his claws into were screaming in agony. I began coughing blood—the red liquid causing a spark of delight in his beady eyes.

"Why do you fight me, Sofia? Why do you resist?" he asked as I scampered away from him, backing myself up into a wall. He dipped his finger in the blood on the floor and licked it. He closed his eyes. "There's nothing like it. What is it that makes your blood so delightfully sweet?"

I wanted to glare up at him but one of my eyes was already swollen shut. I was trying to figure out a way to retrieve the wooden stake I kept strapped round my thigh without Borys noticing.

Maybe I'm doing this the wrong way. Perhaps I should play along with his game and pretend to want him so I can stab him in the heart while he's having his way with me. I grimaced. The very idea of his hands on me made me sick.

"Are you not tired, Sofia?" He tilted his head to the side, a smirk forming on his face.

Exhausted. I returned his smirk. "The disgust I feel looking at you is enough to give me all the energy I need. Just the sight of you makes my skin crawl."

His stocky, muscular build tensed. My words had struck a chord.

"Take that back," he growled.

Should I prod on with my insults, he would hurt me some more, but inside, I was also hoping that it would somehow repel him to know how much I hated him. "It's true. Have you ever had a woman actually want to be with you? Isn't that why you have to do this? Force us? I am not yours, Borys. I can never enjoy your touch the way I enjoy Derek's. You're not even a fraction of the man he is. That's why you envy him so much."

He grabbed me by the shoulders and I had to scream when he threw me across the room into a wall. I crashed to the ground with a thud and before I could even make a single move, he was on top of me, stuffing his discarded shirt down my throat until I began gagging.

"You have to learn to shut up, Sofia, my pet. Say such foul things again and I will cut your tongue out... and heal you... and then cut it out again." He pressed a hand over one of my broken ribs, making me scream through his shirt. "We could end this, Sofia. Just cooperate with me. Pleasure me..."

I couldn't hate anyone more than I hated him at that moment. He made even Lucas, who had dealt me his own share of cruel torment, seem like a gentleman. I clawed at Borys with the strength I had left, but he just knelt over me and laughed as he took hold of both my wrists and pinned them over my head. He used his weight to keep my legs down while he used his free hand to begin unbuttoning my shirt.

He bared his fangs, ready to drink from my exposed neck, forcing my head to the side to allow him better access. I shut my eyes, hoping to escape. I wasn't sure if it was just my imagination when I heard a knock on the door.

"Has it been an hour?" He turned his head toward the door and gave it a cold glare before turning his attention back to me. To my relief, it seemed he'd lost interest in drinking my blood, but he then turned his attention to groping my body.

When another series of knocks came at the door, I didn't even fight the urge to sigh with utter relief. *Please, for mercy's sake, don't stop knocking.*

Upon noticing how relieved I was, Borys decided to take his frustration out on me by grabbing fistfuls of my hair. By doing so, he let go of my wrists, and I clawed at him and hit him.

Annoyed, he forced my arms to my sides before wrapping one strong arm around me to keep me steady as he stood up and freely kissed my neck and jawline. He walked toward the door even as he held me in his arms.

I steeled myself against more tears. I didn't want to cry any longer, but I also had no fight left in me either, so my exhausted form just hung within his embrace. I hoped that whoever was behind that door would provide me momentary relief from Borys

Maslen.

Borys opened the door.

I only realized how terrible I looked when Ingrid, whom I was certain didn't give a damn about me, gasped. "What have you done to her? Are you trying to kill her?"

Borys pulled his mouth away from my cheek. "She's trying to kill herself with all the fight she's putting up. Little minx can't seem to get it in her head that she's mine."

"Lest you forget, she's the only leverage you have against Derek Novak. If you destroy her, you're not leaving this island alive."

Borys scoffed. "Just one drink of my blood will fix her."

"Let her drink mine."

I was stunned to hear the familiar voice. *Vivienne.* She stepped into the room right behind Ingrid.

"What's *she* doing here?" Borys spat out, though none of us missed the way his grip loosened around me as he perused Vivienne from head to foot. There was no mistaking that he still wanted Vivienne after all those years.

"A gift from Derek Novak." Ingrid shrugged.

"I'll do anything you want me to." Vivienne looked confident enough, but her voice broke when she spoke the words. "Just stop tormenting Sofia."

Borys grinned as he wrapped both his arms around me, crushing my broken ribs against his firm chest. "Hear that, Sofia? Your lover is so enamored by you that he would willingly whore out his own sister just to rescue you."

I hate you. With all the defiance I still had left within me, I spat in his face. Angered, he threw me to the ground. Vivienne rushed to my side.

"Sofia, you look awful," she muttered under her breath. She bit into her wrist and made me drink her blood.

"What do you think you're doing?" Borys fisted a clump of Vivienne's hair.

"Healing her. If I don't, she will die. Do you not see how much you've broken her?" Vivienne responded through gritted teeth. "I can barely see a trace of her original complexion. She's black, purple and blue."

"Serves her right for not giving in to me." Borys walked away from us and leaned against the wall, arms crossed over his chest as he watched Vivienne feed me more of her blood.

The momentary reprieve was exactly what I needed as my eyes met Vivienne's. Her blue-violet gaze bore into mine with sympathy and compassion. She was the one person I knew who had been in Borys' cruel hands before, which was why I was so shocked when she said, "Just give in to him, Sofia. Let him have his way. There's no point in fighting back. You'll only get hurt worse if you don't give in."

I stared up at her in horror. *She must know how disgusted I am by his touch, how revolted I am whenever I sense his eyes on me. How could she ask this of me?* Her own memories—ones that she had shared with me before—flooded through my mind. How she'd fought back with everything that she was until her mind snapped. It had taken years before she'd recovered.

"That's what I'm talking about." Borys reveled in her words. "You should listen to Vivienne, Sofia. She knows. If Derek hadn't taken her away from me, Vivienne and I would've gotten along well even to this very moment. Isn't that right, Vivienne?"

Vivienne didn't respond. She checked on me and seemed

satisfied that I was healing fine. I could see the fear in her eyes and I gulped at what she was planning to do. She rose to her feet and faced Borys.

It finally dawned on me what she was doing. She was using herself as bait. My heart broke at the sacrifice she was making for me.

Vivienne approached Borys slowly, taking her time. Caught in her spell, he remained still, devouring her with his eyes. I couldn't help but sneer at how delighted he seemed. I was certain that no woman had ever given him the same attention Vivienne was giving him at that moment.

She caressed his face and hair. She pressed her lips against his jaw. A sigh of pleasure escaped Borys' lips. The pleasure he was taking from Vivienne's humiliation sickened me.

He grabbed her by the waist and pulled her body against his before turning so that Vivienne's back was against the wall. Now having a pliable victim, he seemed to revel in the idea that Vivienne was just going to let him do whatever he pleased.

I rose to my feet, my eyes on Vivienne. She looked straight at me even as Borys began ripping the neckline of her shirt and kissing her collarbone. *What am I waiting for? This is my chance.* I reached for the wooden stake attached to my thigh and slipped it out. Vivienne's eyes widened and she raised one hand to motion for me to wait.

To my shock, she began running her hands over his bare torso and slightly tugged at his jeans to lower them. *What is she doing?*

"Borys is good to those who are good to him, isn't that right?" Vivienne said, and Borys moaned his agreement as he gripped her hips and lifted her up higher against the wall, his own hips supporting her weight. "Let me teach Sofia how to please you. You'll like it when she learns."

He hesitated. I was afraid that he was going to turn and find the wooden stake in my hand, so I hid it behind my back as I approached them. But Vivienne continued to coax him. "You'll have us both. Isn't that what you want?"

It sickened me, and I sped up my steps toward him. I was about a foot away when Vivienne nodded.

"Let me down, Borys," she pleaded after she kissed him.

His head was probably still reeling from her kiss, because he lowered her to the ground. Vivienne continued to kiss him. "Turn around, baby... Sofia is right behind you and I'm going to instruct her on what to do so that you won't get so mad at her all the time."

He must've been expecting kisses from me—evident from the look of euphoria on his face as he spun around to face me.

By the time he saw the stake, it was already driven deep into his heart.

He staggered on his feet before Vivienne held his jaw from behind and swiftly snapped his neck.

Just like that, the great Borys Maslen dropped to the ground, dead.

I couldn't believe my eyes. We'd done it. Vivienne and I had defeated Borys Maslen.

As much as I was relieved, however, I could feel pain in my heart. *This is what it feels like to end the life of another.* Overwhelmed, I did the only thing I could. I broke down in tears, and so did Vivienne.

I didn't know exactly what caused her tears, but I liked to

believe that we were crying over the same thing. We were crying over the many lives lost, the many broken souls, the many more that would be lost and broken in the days to come.

Chapter 50: Derek

The silence was worse than the bangs and the screams. It left too much room for my mind to concoct images of what Borys was putting Sofia through. *And now Vivienne's at his mercy too.*

"They've been quiet for too long. What's going on in there? I can't stand this." I began marching toward the room.

"What do you think you're doing?" Aiden motioned to stop me. "That monster might kill Sofia."

"Do you hear that silence, Aiden? She might be dead already!" I choked on the words. "We're going in."

Unlike Aiden, they knew me well enough not to protest, so they just nodded and we began to walk toward the corridor that led to the room. The corridor was guarded by Borys' minions.

"What do you think you're doing?" Ingrid got in my way.

"You know for a fact that I can destroy you, Ingrid," I snarled. "Since you've made it quite clear how indifferent you are to Sofia,

I don't think she'll mind my killing you either, so get out of my way."

"Borys will kill my daughter the moment you walk through that door."

"Your daughter?" I hissed. "You talk as if you care about what happens to her."

"Don't do anything rash," she warned.

"Let me talk to him…"

She gave it a moment's thought and looked at the vampires standing behind me. She nodded and motioned for me to follow her.

As we walked past the other vampires, I couldn't help but feel something was amiss. It almost felt as if they were looking at me with admiration. One of them particularly caught my eye. A man would have to be blind to not notice how gorgeous she looked. Our eyes locked and I knew without a doubt that she too was attracted to me.

I swallowed hard, guilty that I was checking out another woman—an enemy at that—while Sofia was most likely going through hell. *What's wrong with you, Novak?*

I followed Ingrid into the room and practically bumped into her when she stopped in her tracks. I side-stepped her and my jaw dropped. Borys' dead body lay on the ground and a broken and bruised Sofia sobbed next to him. Vivienne was sitting a couple of feet away from Sofia, looking distraught.

I couldn't understand what was going on. I was wrought with a mixture of shock, joy and confusion.

Before Ingrid, frozen with shock, could gather her wits about her, I rushed toward Sofia, making sure that she was safe. "Take them all captive! Now! Kill them if you have to!"

Chaos erupted outside the room. Ingrid threw herself at Borys' body, her entire form racked with sobs. I embraced Sofia, unable to bear looking at the bruises—slowly healing—all over her body.

"Are you all right?" I whispered into her ear, tightening my embrace around her, feeling her tremble against my body.

She nodded into my shoulder.

"You did it, Sofia. I don't know how, but you ended Borys Maslen."

"They might need you out there..." she whispered hoarsely.

I knew she was right, so I pulled away from her. I directed my attention toward Vivienne. "Keep an eye on Ingrid. Keep her away from Sofia." Satisfied, I stepped out of the room to find all of the other vampires dead. All but one—the beautiful brunette who had caught my eye earlier as I'd passed her by...

She glared at me, eyes blazing—this time with anger.

"You've no idea what you've done." She shook her head at me even as she motioned to attack me. She was being held back by Xavier and Sam.

I narrowed my eyes. I knew by instinct that she could've easily gotten out of their grips if she wanted to. "Who are you?" I asked.

"You don't remember, do you?"

"Remember what?"

"Emilia. I'm Emilia. You made a huge mistake today, Derek, but don't worry... you'll get back on track soon enough. For now, I'm warning you. He won't stop until he gets a hold of her."

"He? Who's he?" I tightened my jaw. "I don't even care. Let him know that he will never get a hold of Sofia. I will wage war on anybody who threatens her."

"I'm going to forgive this momentary lapse of your sanity, Derek. I don't understand how you of all people have come under her spell, but you'll snap out of it eventually." She looked at me with a lingering, sultry gaze. "Don't act like you don't know what I'm talking about. You felt the attraction immediately, didn't you? You felt what I felt."

"I have no idea what you're talking about," I lied, swallowing back my guilt. "You're delusional."

She chuckled. "You don't belong with her, Derek Novak. You belong with me."

I straightened to my full height. "I don't even know who you are."

"Of course you do." She smiled. "I'm a daughter of the darkness just as surely as you are his son."

"*His?*"

"The original. He meant you for me."

Before the words could even sink in, she vanished before my eyes.

My knees buckled beneath me. No matter how much I tried to deny it, Emilia had something about her that just drew me to her. Like we were somehow connected...

"Derek?"

Sofia stood by the door. I wondered if she had heard what Emilia had just said. "Sofia..." The words came out in a whisper.

"Who was that?" she asked. "How was that possible? She just... disappeared."

I didn't know how to respond. "I don't know. I've never seen her before." Sofia approached me and I pulled her against me, reassured that I loved her deeply and that even my attraction for another woman could never shake that love. Still, my attraction to Emilia was killing me, and I couldn't understand why.

"What just happened? No one just disappears like that..." Xavier spoke up.

"If she is who she says she is, then we're at war with a force far greater than just the other vampire covens or the hunters," Vivienne said, emerging from the room.

I nodded. "We need to prepare for war."

"We wouldn't have to do that if the cure works," Sofia said.

At that, I couldn't help but scoff as everyone turned toward Aiden, who, with downcast eyes, had to tell his own daughter that he'd been playing her all along.

I hated how much it broke Sofia's heart when he said, "There is no cure."

CHAPTER 51: SOFIA

I snuggled close to Derek on the couch inside the octagonal room at the top of the Lighthouse. All the candles inside the room were lit and we were surrounded by silence.

I wondered how it was possible that Derek and I could have such dysfunctional parents. Both of mine were now captives of The Shade and, as much as I loved Aiden, I couldn't bring myself to feel any sympathy for him.

Derek began brushing his thumb over my shoulder blade as he pressed his lips against my temple. "What's on your mind, Sofia?"

"My father," I responded. "My crazy mother... Us..."

"Us?"

I sat up and spun around to face him, kneeling on the couch so that I could look directly into his handsome face. "Do you still want to marry me?" My voice broke as the question came out. I touched the diamond pendant he had given me for my birthday.

His blue eyes softened. "Of course I do, Sofia. You know I do."

"You're immortal."

I waited for his usual assurances. I was expecting him to tell me that what we had was worth fighting for and that there had to be a way. Instead, all I got was silence.

Perhaps the reality of it all is finally sinking in to him. There's no way we can be together.

The idea that Aiden had played me, that he had used me to get to Derek, was still breaking my heart, but I didn't want to cry over it. Mostly, I felt anger toward my father for doing that to me.

"Derek, please say something."

"I don't know what to say," he admitted and I saw tears in his eyes.

"So that's it, I guess..." My shoulders sagged with resignation. "We really can't be together?"

Anger contorted the features of his face. "What? Sofia, what are you saying?" He cupped my cheeks with both hands. "You're talking nonsense. We belong together."

I knew what he was saying was true, but it was easy to give in to despair. "How does this work, Derek?"

His eyes darkened. I wondered what was going through his mind. I wished I could read his thoughts.

After a long silence, I began shaking my head. "There has got to be a cure." I couldn't bring myself to accept that this was no longer a possibility.

"You can't cure a curse, Sofia. It's not a disease."

"How could there not be one, Derek? I'm supposed to be a vampire! And yet here I am... Can someone be immune from a curse?"

He paused before shrugging. "I don't know."

"Let's say there isn't a cure. What then is true sanctuary? What's going to happen from here on out, Derek? Not just with us... I mean the island... everything."

"Don't ask me what true sanctuary is, Sofia. I fought for it for an entire century, practically gave up my soul for it. I thought I already had sanctuary after establishing The Shade, only to find out that I didn't... I just don't understand the prophecy. What I do know is that war is brewing. That's what's going to happen."

"So that's it? More bloodshed?"

"Did you really believe there was ever any other way?"

"I don't think this is the way."

"Well, it's the only way unless you find this cure." He gripped my shoulders. "I hope you know how much I want this to be true, Sofia. I want that cure more than anybody else, but until we find it, I need you to be with me no matter what comes our way. I need you by my side."

I leaned forward and kissed him. Gentle. Calm. Reassuring. I whispered in his ear. "I'm with you, Derek. I'm right here with you."

"Always?"

"For as long as I have breath."

EPILOGUE: VIVIENNE

I was in the middle of a battlefield. There were bone-chilling screams, and blood from both humans and vampires streamed through the site... There were no victors, just victims, most of whom were innocent.

Suddenly, the battlefield was swept away in a dark vortex and I found myself in the middle of a great hall. Decking the walls were large portraits that honored the fallen. Chills ran down my spine when I recognized some of the faces in the pictures. The Hudsons, the family that had taken Sofia in when Aiden had abandoned her. The Hendrys, Cameron and Liana's descendants. Adults and children alike... lost.

My mind was still reeling when I was once again swept away into another scene—one of the most painful and agonizing things I'd ever witnessed.

Derek Novak was being forced into the cruel rays of the sun, screaming in pain as he burned to his death... Sofia stood in the background, staring helplessly, tears rushing down her cheeks. Her eyes found mine and the moment our gazes locked, everything faded away.

I snapped out of the vision, blinking several times before getting full control of my faculties. One thought was circling my mind as I began to shiver at the horrors I had just witnessed.

If we are to survive, we must find the cure.

Ready for the next part of
Derek and Sofia's story?

A Shade of Vampire 5: A Blaze of Sun is available now!

Visit www.bellaforrest.net for more information.

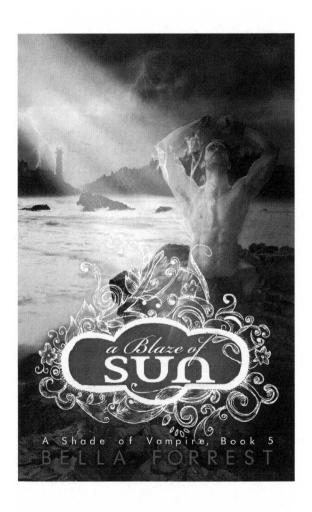

If you want to stay updated about my latest book releases, join my VIP list! Visit: www.forrestbooks.com, enter your email address and you'll be the first to know when the next book is released.

Love,
Bella x

P.S. Also, don't forget to come say hello on Facebook. I'd love to meet you personally:
www.facebook.com/AShadeOfVampire

P.P.S. You can also say hi to me on Twitter: @ashadeofvampire
And Instagram: @ashadeofvampire

Made in the USA
Lexington, KY
27 June 2016